I0666180

The Cell's Door

First Edition

Nigel Cross

The Cell's Door

First Edition

Published by The Nazca Plains Corporation
Las Vegas, Nevada
2006

ISBN: 978-1-887895-79-8

Published by

The Nazca Plains Corporation ®
4640 Paradise Rd, Suite 141
Las Vegas NV 89109-8000

PUBLISHER'S NOTE
The Cell's Door is a work of fiction created wholly by *Nigel Cross's*
imagination. All characters are fictional and any resemblance to
any persons living or deceased is purely by accident. No portion
of this book reflects any real person or events.

Cover Photo and Art Direction, Blake Stephens

Dedication

To Plato, who never let a word of Socrates go unwritten

To Nietzsche, who never let a word of Socrates go unforgiven

The Cell's Door

Nigel Cross

Contents

Chapter I ——————————————— 11

Chapter II ——————————————— 17

Chapter III ——————————————— 21

Chapter IV ——————————————— 25

Chapter V ——————————————— 33

Chapter VI ——————————————— 37

Chapter VII ——————————————— 41

Chapter VIII ——————————————— 47

Chapter IX ——————————————— 51

Chapter X ——————————————— 57

Chapter XI ——————————————— 61

Chapter XII ——————————————— 71

Chapter XIII ——————————————— 77

Chapter XIV ——————————————— 85

Chapter XV ——————————————— 97

Chapter XVI ——————————————— 105

Chapter XVII ——————————————— 113

Chapter XVII ——————————————— 123

Chapter XIX ——————————————— 131

Chapter XX ——————————————— 141

Chapter XXI ——————————————— 151

Chapter XXII ——————————————— 163

Chapter XXIII ——————————————— 169

About the Author ——————————————— 177

Chapter I

Mere survival is an affliction.
What is of interest is life, and the direction of that life.
Guy Fregault

Once made equal to man, woman becomes his superior.
Socrates

Not all cells have steel bars. Some are designed to simulate comfort, even to the point that they are no longer recognized as what they really are: a place to confine those subjected to a loss of freedom. From the damp hovels of ancient Mesopotamia to the corporate board rooms of Los Angeles, the misty shroud of destitution breathed its gripping hold in a clasp of hopelessness, never surrendering its control even to the passage of millenia.

David Bruester knew nothing of the life of the Mesopotamian prisoner, but he always sensed something was wrong. Getting up at six o'clock in the morning to run three miles, driving through snail-paced, rush-hour traffic, scanning reports for errors before passing them onto superiors who simulated his earlier actions, keeping order in a random work environment of a stock brokerage firm, and then making the journey home again to allow a slight reprieve from his indentured status before beginning the whole process over again, was his way of life. For years, he had no reason to complain; he grew used to the way and never questioned it.

There was a strange smile on David Bruester's face when he dumped his briefcase on his desk and pressed the intercom on his telephone. "Maggie," he said, "I need you to confirm my reservations for tonight."

A friendly voice replied. "Already done, sir. You leave for San Francisco at six o'clock this evening."

"Thank you," he said as he sat down in his chair.

"Mr. Bruester," said Maggie's voice, "Mr. Thompson left a message with me to have you call him as soon as you arrived to work."

A smile came to Bruester's face. <u>One more time. That's all I have to take.</u> "Thank you, Maggie. I'll call him."

Dominique Schauer entered her office and was only there a second before her secretary, a young man in his early twenties, looked up to see her. "Sleeping on the job, Robert?" she said with a smile.

His eyes showed his fear. The last thing in the world he wanted was to have Dominique Schauer suspect he had been sleeping on the job. He didn't fear being fired, because that would probably never happen. His only fear was that he might displease his employer, and he would do anything to avoid that. That was much worse than being fired. "No, Miss Schauer. I was thinking about your proposal to the board. I wanted to insure you had a typed copy before the meeting."

She nodded. "Then insure that I do."

"Yes, Ma'am," he said as he went back to his typewriter, even though he didn't type anything. He wanted perfection before he put anything on paper. That was the way it had to be.

Dominique entered her private office and closed the door behind her. She liked Robert. He was efficient, and he loved to work for her. As a matter of fact, he practically worshipped her, and he did come cheap. Dominique doubted that many corporate decision makers had labor working for them at such cheap prices. That was the one advantage of Dominique's chosen lifestyle. Assistants just seemed to pile up, and they did it at unbelievable prices. Robert's salary was just enough to keep him housed and healthy, little else.

Of course, Dominique also controlled Robert's entire social life. It was that fact that kept Robert in her employ; he lived for the opportunity to be near her, as did everyone of the employees in her care. Robert, like the rest of them, lived to make her life just a bit more pleasant. That was the way it was supposed to be, and she knew it.

"Robert," said Dominique into her intercom. "Come into my office."

A second later, the door opened and Robert entered. He walked to the front of her desk and stood at attention. She looked him over and then smiled. "We are alone, Robert. Is that how you present yourself?"

Robert took a deep breath and then dropped to his knees. "I ask your forgiveness, Mistress."

Dominique smiled. "No apology necessary, my slave. I have been liberal with you in order for you to serve as my personal secretary. In order to avoid embarrassing me in front of the rest of the corporate world, you have been granted the honor of addressing me as a secretary would to his employer, calling me Miss Schauer instead of Mistress at all times. However, you must remember to present yourself properly whenever you are alone in my presence."

"Yes, Mistress," said Robert as he dropped his head to the carpeted floor.

"I need you to confirm the flight of my new slave," she said. "It is scheduled for a six o'clock departure, and it should arrive at SFO at seven o'clock."

"I will verify it, Mistress," said Robert quickly.

"I know you will," she said. "Have Gretta pick him up at the airport. He needs to know what is in store for him when he arrives."

"Mistress, shall I tell Gretta to bring the new slave to the compound?"

Dominique stared at her secretary for a long time before speaking. "What makes you think you have permission to instruct Gretta on anything, slave? Gretta is a mistress in training. You are a male, and you are way out of line."

"I apologize, Mistress."

"Not good enough," she said as she opened her desk drawer and pulled out a leather whip with multiple leather tails swaying from its handle. "Mistress Gretta will be bringing the new slave to the training grounds. This is a special case. He has already signed the papers releasing him into my servitude. He is now my property." She swung the whip through the air quickly before she stood up and pointed at her secretary. "Close that door and prop yourself on my desk. Do it now!"

He did it, and he did it quickly. That was the way things were in the employ of Mistress Dominique Schauer.

David stood before Adam Thompson and almost found himself laughing when he received the lecture from his boss. "The Simpson report was totally inadequate," he said, not even looking up from his desk. "The profit margin should have been at least ten percent higher than it was. How am I supposed to explain this to Lawrence Simpson?"

David smiled. "Lawrence Simpson wanted a safe bet. He knew he was going to yield at 13%."

Thompson sighed. "You could have done so much more for that account. Breaking even is not how we do things here."

David shook his head. "Sir, I've already discussed this with Mr. Simpson, and he was pleased with the 13% rating. I offered him several other options, but he wanted to keep his options safe. That is exactly what I did."

Thompson stared back down at his desk. "How are your other accounts?"

"Everything is caught up until the end of the fiscal year," said David.

"Everything?" said Thompson. "Nothing is ever completely caught up."

David took a deep breath and then let it out. "Is there something you're trying to tell me, sir?"

He nodded. "I believe you've chosen a very inopportune time to take a vacation. San Francisco, isn't it?"

"Yes, sir."

He closed the folder that was on his desk. "I'm afraid that I have to disapprove your leave of absence. I can't afford to have you out of this office for the entire two weeks you have coming on your vacation."

A smile crossed David's face. "I never put in for vacation, sir."

Thompson pulled a folder out from his desk and looked it over. "No, you didn't, did you? How were you planning to take this vacation without using vacation time? You know the company requires you to remain local during your weekends."

He took a deep breath and then let it out. "I'm not coming back from this trip."

The words sunk into Thompson's head. "What?"

"You heard me," said David. "When I leave for San Francisco tonight, I do not intend to come back."

Thompson's anger switched to astonishment. "Are you quitting?"

"Yes, sir. I am."

"You can't quit! You didn't give your two week notice."

"Then fire me," said David with a smile as he turned to exit the office.

"You'll never work in this field again if you walk out that door," said Thompson. "I can make your life miserable if I decide to."

David turned back and stared at Thompson. "My life ends when I board that plane to San Francisco. Our paths will never cross again."

Thompson just watched as David exited the office and slammed the door shut behind him. He couldn't think of a response that was appropriate to the situation. There just didn't seem to be one.

Chapter II

When David stepped off the plane, he found himself wondering if he was doing the right thing. This was something he fantasized about since he was old enough to remember, and he was sure that he wanted it more than anything else. However, when the opportunity finally presented itself as reality, he was beginning to wonder if his choice for the future was wise. After all, what did he know about this woman anyway?

He knew she was a mistress in charge of slaves; that was attracted him to her in the first place. In his many letters and phone calls to her, he opened himself to her and told her his secret fantasies. It came as such a pleasant surprise to him when she wasn't shocked by his desire to be controlled by a powerful woman. As a matter of fact, she accepted it as a normal circumstance, as if it shouldn't have been any other way.

"Are you David?" said a soft voice from behind him. He whirled around to see a short, brown-haired woman in a business suit. She smiled when he made eye contact with her. "David Bruester?" she said.

He nodded quickly, not sure of what to say. He expected someone to pick him up, but he assumed it would have been one of Mistress Dominique's male slaves, not a woman. He didn't even know how to address her.

"I am Mistress Trainee Gretta," she said. "You will address me as such. Do you understand, David?"

He looked around and realized there were people close enough to them who could actually hear what she said. An older woman appeared very interested in his response. "Yes, I understand."

Gretta smiled and then shook her head slowly. "Slave, you have a lot of training ahead of you. Follow me."

He followed close behind her and realized she was heading for the exit. "Uh, Mistress Trainee Gretta, I need to get my bags before we leave."

She stopped walking and turned to face him. "Slave, there are some rules you need to be aware of before we continue. First of all, you never address a woman unless you have permission to speak. Is that understood?"

"Yes," he said. "I understand."

She sighed. "Yes, what?"

He thought quickly. "Yes, Mistress."

She sighed again. "Try again."

"Yes, Mistress Trainee Gretta."

"That's better," she said. Before he could say anything else, she turned and walked towards the terminal's exit.

"Uh, Mistress Trainee Gretta, may I please have your permission to speak."

She continued walking but turned to him in a manner that suggested she wasn't too interested in anything he had to say. "Make it quick. I don't like too many words from a slave."

"Mistress Trainee Gretta, may I get my bags before we leave? All of my clothes are in them."

They reached a black limousine that was being guarded by a man in a black suit. "Mistress Trainee Gretta," said the man as he quickly opened the back door of the vehicle and stood aside to allow her to enter. She stepped into the car and motioned for David to follow behind her.

David stood in place for a moment, wondering what he was supposed to do about all of his clothing. He couldn't just leave it at the airport. Someone might steal it.

"Get in the car!" said Gretta as she took a seat on a plush chair that was on the other side away from the door. "Don't make me have to raise my voice. You wouldn't like that."

Quickly, David jumped into the car and took a seat on the plush chair that appeared to stretch in a circle around the limousine. Taking a quick look around, he could see a refrigerator, a television set, a mobile phone, and many other little attachment items that appeared to bring a sense of luxury to the expensive limousine. His eyes kept taking in the plush atmosphere until he felt a shove on his shoulder, and he fell to the floor of the limousine.

"Slaves don't sit in chairs," she said to him. "Slaves remain on the floor where they belong. Is that understood?"

David nodded slowly. He was beginning to wonder if this was really something he wanted to do. Even as that thought entered his head, Gretta slapped him hard across the face. "You never answer a question without addressing the woman in words. Is that understood?"

"Yes, Mistress Trainee Gretta," he said.

"Good," she said. "Now, as for your bags, don't worry about them. From this time forward, you own nothing. If your mistress decides you are to have possession of something, that is her choice. She owns you."

An aching feeling started crawling through David's system as the vehicle began moving forward. "Mistress Trainee Gretta, may I have permission to speak?"

"No," she said. "I don't want to hear anything more from you. Why don't you take off my shoes and massage my feet for me, slave?"

He stared at her and then decided he had to speak his mind. "Mistress Trainee Gretta, I don't think I'm ready for all this. I thought I was, but I'm not sure anymore."

She stared into his eyes and shook her head. "Did I give you permission to speak?"

He stared up at her. "Didn't you hear what I said?"

Gretta stared at her fingernails and examined her professional manicure as she spoke. "Mistress Dominique owns you. You cannot back out of your slavery now." She allowed herself a powerful grin. "So get my damn shoes off and start massaging my feet before I skin you alive!"

Without a second thought, he pulled off her high heels and began to do as ordered. He was beginning to realize that there was little choice of what exactly he was supposed to do.

After all, that was supposedly what he always wanted.

Chapter III

The trip seemed to take forever; at least that's how it felt to David. He never imagined there was so much involved in a foot massage. After all, it was just a foot; how could there be so much involved in massaging it. You just rub it continuously until you've pleased the owner. Wasn't that the way it was supposed to be?

Well, not according to Mistress Trainee Gretta. Everytime he thought he had it right, she would tell him to stop and start over, explaining that he wasn't pressing hard enough, wasn't seeking out the sensitive areas rather than just rubbing over them and moving onto other spots. She explained that he needed to understand how to feel the foot and know where exactly it needed to be rubbed harder and softer by the feel of the muscles underneath. Each time he tried to explain that he didn't understand what she meant, and she would just correct him and tell him to do it over again. In what should have been a fifteen minute foot massage, in David's opinion, turned out to be about a two hour foot massage that left David's hands very tired by the time they finally reached the place where Mistress Dominique lived.

Upon their arrival, Mistress Trainee Gretta dropped her feet off of David's lap and to the floor of the limousine. "Well, slave, you're home."

Nervousness passed over David, the kind of nervousness he couldn't ever remember experiencing before. In his short life, he lived in a business atmosphere that was high-pressure, at least according to his analyst, but this was the first time he ever experienced feelings like this. It wasn't just a fear of the unknown; it was an inner dread that told him that he was about to step into an endless pit that would continue consuming him for the rest of his life, if not for eternity. And there was nothing he could do but step into the pit and face that endless chasm.

He thought of running. There was still time for him to change all of this. Sure, it was a hot fantasy, but this was about to become real. He was surrendering everything he had ever known, and he was going to be totally at the whim of another individual, someone who wouldn't hesitate to punish him if he was ever in error. And judging from the training he had received from her in the past, he knew that error was a common occurrence in her world. There was just no pleasing this woman. And when she punished, she was quite vicious in her techniques and seemed to relish the horror that she spread to her various slaves.

Yes, he could run. Mistress Trainee Gretta might be an obstacle here, but he tended to believe that she couldn't stop him if he really wanted to get away. Sure, the driver would probably try to stop him, but he even suspected that the driver wouldn't be able to stop him if he really wanted to escape. Yes, that seemed to be a viable option.

"Slave, you seem to be thinking about something," said Mistress Trainee Gretta. "What is it?"

He stared at her but said nothing.

With lightening speed, she slapped him across the face. "A question from me is not a request, slave. Your thoughts are no longer your own. If I ask for them, you give them. Now, what were you thinking?

He thought quickly. "Mistress Trainee Gretta, I am sorry. I was just thinking about how scared I am."

She slapped him across the face again. "You're lying!"

He just stared back at her.

"Slave, do you honestly believe you're the first person to come here under such circumstances? You're wondering if perhaps you made a mistake, if maybe you should have just run instead of coming." She allowed herself a smile. "You're wondering if you should try to escape, aren't you?

David was too embarrassed to answer. Yes, he had wanted to escape. He seemed to want that more than anything. The rest didn't matter anymore. He didn't want this. This was his freedom he was about to give up, and the last thing in the world he wanted to do was talk about it. He just wanted to run.

"Well, slave, let me just warn you of the foolishness of such thoughts." She pointed in the direction of the main house that was surrounded by a very large metal fence. "Once inside, you won't escape. That barbed wire on the fence has cut more than one slave in the past. And it's quite willing to do the same to any future one who is stupid enough to try to escape."

He decided not to mention that he was probably going to be gone before he ever made it through the gate that connected to that fence, so the thought of barbed wire really didn't mean a lot to him.

"And, slave, if you're thinking of escaping before you enter, think again. The house is the only place within twenty miles of civilization, and there are cameras throughout the countryside that will insure that you don't make it far before you are brought back by a very extensive and well-trained staff. And even if you were able to make it to civilization, you would never be safe. Mistress Dominique takes her slavery contracts very seriously. It might take her a long time, but she would hunt you down and find you no matter where you went. She has a lot of assets at her disposal that you can't possibly imagine. When you chose to be her slave, you chose well, but you also chose foolishly if you ever thought you might be able to get out of this contract."

He thought about the contract. It was for a year, and it would automatically be extended yearly as long as she was pleased with his service. In other words, she was the only one who could release him. Otherwise, he was a slave for the rest of his life.

He nodded slowly.

"Very well," said Mistress Trainee. "Now, I think you've worn your clothing long enough. From this moment on, you are to exist in the clothing the Goddess allowed you when you first entered her world. Strip, now!"

Quickly, he stripped off his clothing and started to fold it neatly.

"Don't worry about folding it!" she said. "When we incinerate your clothing, it doesn't matter how neat it was before it burns. Now, on your knees."

David dropped to his knees, constantly wondering where people find limousines that are big enough to practically stand in. As he knelt, his body shook in fear; he wasn't ready for this, and he knew it.

She reached into a compartment of the limousine and pulled out a set of handcuffs that she forced onto his wrists, locking his hands behind his back. Then she pulled out a larger set of shackles, and pushed his chest so he fell off balance and onto his behind. Before he could even think of protesting, she starting shackling the manacles onto his legs, and was done in only a few seconds, locking padlocks onto the shackles. There didn't seem to be any keys in the nearby vicinity. "Just in case you still might have any stupid ideas," she said with a smile.

Then the door was opened from behind him and he felt himself being dragged out of the car. It only took a second to realize it was the driver who said nothing but propped David up on his feet and then went back to the car. Mistress Trainee Gretta exited the car after him and then smiled at David. "Now, slave, I think it's time you meet your new owner. Follow me, and don't keep me waiting. My promise to skin you alive still stands."

She started walking towards the main gate, and he tried to follow close behind her, although the very small chain between the two shackles on his leg made it quite difficult.

Chapter IV

David hobbled his way through the main gate before he stopped in his tracks, even though he was being hustled forward by Mistress Trainee Gretta. He knew he didn't have a choice in the matter, that he was going through that gate no matter what happened, but as he stood there naked and chained, he took a second to look around and realized that this was much more serious than he would have normally desired. For some reason unknown to him, he couldn't even move. He was stuck in place.

Mistress Trainee Gretta stopped walking, realized that he was not trying to keep up with her anymore, and then she walked back to him, a riding crop very present in sight. "I'm only going to say this to you once, slave. You don't have a choice here. You are a slave, and you WILL follow me into the house." She moved real close to him, so that her hot breath was all over him. "You do understand that, don't you, slave?"

He was too scared to answer.

But she didn't hit him. To his surprise, she started to laugh. "Slave, you are not the first to regret your decision you probably made while thinking about the numerous hard-ons you were going to have while here. Did you honestly believe it would be one big fantasy game after another with you getting your rocks off every fifteen minutes?" She started laughing even harder. "It happens to all of you, slave, so don't think you're any different. Even the women who come here have their own illusions, or possibly delusions, of what is going to happen here, and once it does, they get very scared and beg to leave." She grasped his hair and pulled him forward, practically throwing him to his knees on the dirt walkway; he could feel the stones and rocks cutting into his skin, grating and slashing his skin. "Slave, consider yourself lucky. Your regrets are coming even before you step through the main gate. But once you signed that contract, you signed away your life, and there is no mercy, or pity, for one such as you." Then she laughed again. "And don't think for an instant that I care one way or another whether you are happy or frightened." She pulled him back to his feet by his hair. Then she spoke again. "Actually, I take that back. I do care, but you'll discover that I'm with the majority when I feel that I'd rather have you frightened than scared." She smiled in delight. "There's nothing like the sight of a frightened, whimpering slave. Well, that's not true either. A frightened, whimpering slave in pain is better." Then she turned away and started walking towards the house. "But that's for later. I'm sure you'll find out all about that."

He followed closer behind her this time, even though the chains on his ankles made it very difficult for him to maneuver forward very far. He tried, but he just couldn't keep up the speed she was requiring of him. But he did the best he could; after all, he figured Mistress Trainee Gretta would demand nothing less.

A million thoughts were going through his head. Was this what he really wanted? Had he made a horrible mistake? Was he truly submissive enough for such an experience as this? How many tickets would they give his car before they finally towed it off the street where he left it? Was Charmin really the softest bathroom tissue on the market?....

Just then, he heard the sound of clanking metal and then a very abrupt metal crash. He whirled around in a bit of a panic only to see that the gate that once held him from the house was now the gate that was holding him from any chance of freedom. There was a woman at the gate who locked the gate behind her, giving David a smile in his direction as she indicated with her actions that there was no way possible for him to ever escape because she knew from experience that no one escaped once she locked that gate. That simple knowledge gave her a lot of pleasure and the many prisoners who inhabited this complex over the years a great deal of dread.

Mistress Trainee Gretta turned back to David. "I am going to leave you now, slave." She pointed forward at the one door that was directly in front of them, a door that was placed in the center of the main house, a place where someone would come if being invited to visit. For some reason, David assumed he would be let in the servants' quarters, not the master entrance, but he was not about to ask any questions at this particular point in time. "Enter through that door and embrace your new life."

After Mistress Trainee Gretta disappeared around a far corner of the main entranceway, David walked up the pathway to the main door and took a second before he turned the door handle and pushed the door open. Slowly, he walked into the candlelit room where he stopped for a moment as he pushed the door closed.

It was not a dungeon by any stretch of the imagination; it was a receiving room of sorts, with a very nice plush sofa, red upholstery and carpeting everywhere with numers of candles creating sinister shadows everywhere. There was no manufactured light, just a flickering sensation that hinted the second millenia was hundreds of years from being reached.

He looked around and didn't know what to do. The sofa looked comfortable, and the room was certainly warm enough, but an inner feeling told him that sitting down on that sofa would probably not be a very wise thing to do. He was a slave now, and he needed to know what he could do before he did it. Otherwise, he knew Mistress Dominique well enough to know that she would insure that he never forgot that lesson again.

As a matter of fact, she had taught him that lesson a number of years ago when the two of them had gone to dinner at a fancy restaurant. He was so proud to be at that restaurant with such an elegant woman, the mistress of his dreams, so that after he pulled out her chair and seated her, he hadn't thought a thing about it when he took his own seat. That was when she informed him that he had made a most horrible error by taking the inititative and sitting down without her permission. Until the waiter brought the meal, she had him sit on the floor next to the chair, and when the food was brought, he was instructed to stand up where the chair was and eat standing up. He remembered the confused looks he received from the other patrons in the restaurant and the insultive stares from the staff who thought he was trying to make a spectacle of himself. There were even a couple of people who seemed to understand what was happening, but there were very few of them, and he certainly didn't feel any better realizing that people understood his embarrassment. It was not a good situation for a slave to be in, and he didn't intend to prove that her training had been for nothing on that particular evening.

So, he stood silently with his hands behind his back waiting for his mistress. It was awkward and confusing to be left like this while still fettered and naked, yet he realized this was how his life was going to be from this day forward. There would be no conference calls with New York anymore or frantic investors trying to secure a few more percentage points before the fiscal year ended; all there would be was servitude and orders from a woman who intended to make sure his servitude was not just a joke, but something serious and worthwhile for the two of them.

"So, do you like it?" said a voice from behind him. He turned around slowly to see his mistress standing in the candle light on the other side of the room, having entered through a red doorway that was hidden from the limited light in the room.

He spoke, his voice uneasy as he did. "The room? Yes, Mistress."

She smiled as she stepped closer to him. She was dressed in a red outfit that seemed to be one piece of shiny material from neck to toe. It was so red, and so much a part of this room, that he wondered if she had been in this room all along watching him. He wouldn't put it past her, but then he wondered if that was something she really needed to do. In the past, she had a way of knowing anything he had done wrong, even if she wasn't in the same city, like the time she asked him why he had masturbated without permission when she had started her control over that most secret of functions of his, calling him on his pager at work and telling him that he had permission for the next hour to masturbate, and if he could not break free from whatever obligations that were not a part of her life, he would have to wait until she called him again. Yes, he had failed that one time, and she knew it without even having to ask him. She just phoned him and told him that he would be punished immediately, that she intended him to come to her immediately after work that day. When he arrived, she informed him of his crime, and he was beaten severely for it, even though she never told him how she knew. That was just the way she was.

"Of course, the room," she said with a laugh. "I think it gives a new slave a special feeling whenever he or she enters this room."

David nodded, not knowing what to say in response.

"Regrets, David?" she said.

He took a deep breath but said nothing.

She sighed. "David, when you signed your life over to me, you signed your mind over as well. Remember that line: 'mind, body, and soul'? That was not just for fantasy purposes. I want to know your every thought if I should ask for them. Do you understand?"

"Yes, Mistress," he said.

"Then prove it, David. Regrets?"

He thought quickly and then decided the truth was what she wanted. Besides, if she knew that he was now having problems with his decision, maybe she might let him go, realize that this was all a serious mistake and misunderstanding. "Yes, Mistress. I am having a lot of regrets. I'm so sorry."

She started to laugh. "How cute, David. And you're sorry." Her face suddenly turned serious. "Of course you're sorry. They're all sorry when they realize what it is they've gotten themselves into." She moved closer to him, but her touch didn't appear to be very kind and gentle, like she often was with him. "And now you probably want to leave, having seen a tiny taste of what you're about to receive here. Is that the case, David?"

He took a deep breath and let it out. "Yes, Mistress. I think I made a serious mistake. I don't think I'm ready for this kind of a life."

She was right in front of him now, and she slapped his chest with the palm of her hand, causing little pain but making a lot of sound from her action. "And when will you be, David? When do you think you'll be ready for this kind of life?"

He stared back at her, not knowing what to say.

"So, you'll go back to your stocks and dream of the fantasy of what you might do one day, kind of like you did until you finally took up my offer to become my slave. Do you even have a clue how you'd regret such a decision for the rest your life? Do you even know how many men come to me and beg for such an opportunity?"

He bowed his head in shame. "I'm sorry, Mistress. I realize now I am not worthy of your attentions. I am so sorry to have wasted your time like this. I'm sure those others are much better slaves than I am now."

She started laughing and then put her hands around David's shoulders, drawing him closer to her as she used to do when the two of them were alone in her city dungeon. "You're right, David. You are not worthy of my attentions, but you will be." Her eyes seemed to sparkle as she continued. "Yes, David, you will be worthy of my attentions. Those others might be better slaves than you in that they will do what they have to in order to get in my good graces, but when your training is done, you will be the best slave you can possibly be. Do you under-stand me, David?"

He nodded his head slowly, suddenly realizing that she was not going to be letting him go. "But, Mistress--"

"Silence, slave! You've done enough thinking for that life you just gave up. From now on, I will do the thinking for you. If you think you're not being the best slave you can be, you let me know, and I will decide that for you. If you are not being the best slave you can be, I will make the corrections to make sure that you are. I don't want to hear your thoughts on anything anymore, unless they are of a medical nature, and then you are to tell me everything. I own you now, and you will serve me as I desire. Is that understood, slave?"

"Yes, Mistress," he said slowly.

She started to rub her hands across his chest in very rhythmic circles, enjoying the fact that he was starting to get very aroused. "David, do you remember your safeword when we played in the past? I know you never used it, but do you remember it?"

"Yes, Mistress," he replied. He knew from past experience that he was not to offer any information she did not ask for, so he waited for her to continue the conversation further.

"Well, slave, what is your safeword?"

"It is penguin, Mistress."

She smiled. "It's not anymore."

He looked at her with a bit of confusion in his eyes. It had always been penguin, even though he swore he would never use it, and he never did.

She started to laugh. "Slave, you don't have a safeword anymore. You can tell me when you are feeling severe pain, although I'm sure I'll be able to figure that out from your reactions to what I might do to you. However, I, and I alone, decide when you've had enough or whether or not we are going to go further. Is that understood, slave?"

He didn't know what to say. They had played with that safeword ever since they had had sessions together, even to the point when he stopped being her professional client and started coming around to clean her dungeon in exchange for her control over him. That word was always there between them to save him if things went way too far for him. He didn't know what to do without a safeword.

Her laugh became even more pronounced. "It scares you, doesn't it, slave? No safeword, no limits, no control?"

He nodded his head quickly. "Yes, Mistress."

"Good," she said as she turned to the door on the other side of the room, a black door that didn't try to hide itself as the red door had done before allowing Mistress Dominique to enter the room. "I like my slaves scared. Now, follow me into the house. Your new life is about to begin."

Obediently, he hobbled after her.

Chapter V

He followed close behind her. Because of his experience with Mistress Trainee Gretta, he knew he didn't want to get on the bad side of Mistress Dominique. For everything terrible that Mistress Trainee Gretta might have been, he knew that Mistress Dominique was a thousandfold worse. It was from Mistress Dominique that Mistress Trainee Gretta was learning; it would go without saying that the teacher would be the true entity to fear.

They went through one room after another, not stopping for an instant for him to figure out where they were. It was a rush of colors that they went through, and after only a couple of rooms, he found that he was overwhelmed by the difference in styles and colors of each room. Finally, they came to a black door. But it wasn't the door that caught his attention. What caught his attention was a woman who stood with her hands on her hips and a very wide grin on her face. "Is this him, Headmistress?" she said.

Mistress Dominique nodded slowly. "He is in great need of training. Insure that he learns why he is really here."

"Yes, Headmistress," she said as she turned to David and grabbed him by the hair, pulling him towards her. "Slave, you are to come with me."

David turned to Mistress Dominique, unsure of what to do. He assumed that once he finally came in contact with his mistress, she was going to take control of him. He didn't expect to be turned over to yet another woman.

"Yes, David, you are not ready for me yet." She rubbed his naked arm softly as the other woman pulled him to the door. "This is Mistress Cynthia."

David was scared now. He didn't know this woman. He had intended to serve Mistress Dominique, not someone else. "But, Mistress--"

"But what, slave? Did you think you were ready to serve me properly? Don't you know what an honor it is to finally serve me?"

"But I thought--"

"There you go again, slave. Thinking for yourself. That's why

Mistress Cynthia is here. She will insure you stop doing that. Thinking is very dangerous for a slave, and you are going to learn that. When you come back to me, you will be trained to truly appreciate your station in life."

"But I do, Mistress," he said. "I truly appreciate being your slave."

She laughed. "You think you do, but you should know that being my houseboy is nothing compared to being my slave. You served me in a limited fashion, and that was good for the time, but you have signed on to be my owned property. There's a big difference, and I intend to show you just what that difference is. You have already learned obedience. Now, you will learn true slavery."

David didn't know what to say. He thought he had been through everything he could go through for Mistress Dominique. He thought that was why she had taken him as her personal slave. But obviously, he was wrong. She felt there was more he needed to know, and she intended to make sure he learned that much more.

Mistress Dominique turned to Mistress Cynthia. "He's a treasured piece of property. Treat him as such."

This brought a sense of relief to David until he heard Mistress Cynthia's response. "So, take off the kid gloves?"

"Make it horrible for him," said Mistress Dominique as she turned and walked away. "Let him know what it means to be a slave, and if he lives, bring him back to me."

David's mouth dropped open as Mistress Cynthia pulled him towards the door and then pushed it open. To his surprise, he was led down a gazebo corridor that ran a long length down gardens of the house. For a very long time, the two of them walked, Mistress Cynthia leading the way, down the gazebo corridor until they came to the very end.

Once they left the shade of the gazebo corridor, they were in the open field, and they kept walking. After about ten minutes of walking, David's ankles were really starting to hurt with the manacles on his ankles digging into his flesh. "Mistress, please can I stop for a moment?"

To his surprise, she nodded. Then she pulled out a canteen of water from a bag she was carrying and took a sip of water. Then she turned to him, realizing he was starting to get thirsty himself. "Sorry, slaves don't drink from the same container as mistresses. You'll receive water when we reach our destination."

He nodded slowly, realizing there was not going to be any negotiating with her. Mistresses were strange that way sometimes.

The walk lasted several hours until they were very far from the main house, over a number of hills from it in fact so that it could no longer be seen. Finally, a small structure came into view. As they reached it, it was starting to get dark. It was so hard to believe the first day had come and gone so quickly.

"This is where you will be living for the next while," said Mistress Cynthia. "Get used to it because it will be all that you know. Other than the fields, of course."

David's eyes opened wide. The fields? Was that what was in store for him? The fields? "Is that what I'm to do here, Mistress?" he said.

She walked over to him and slapped him hard across the face. "Haven't you been taught that you don't speak without permission?" David recovered slowly from the blow as she continued speaking. "I let your transgression go before because you were thirsty and probably weren't thinking properly. However, there will be no more mistakes in the future. Is that understood?"

"Yes, Mistress," he said.

She nodded. "In the building is a trough of water. You may drink from there, slave."

He waddled his way into the shed, a run down shelter that was very dark. In a far corner was a trough from which horses probably drank from once. Obediently, and quite thirsty, he knelt down and drank gobs of water that was very warm but cool enough to make him thankful for it. When he finished, he moved around to see Mistress Cynthia standing behind him. "This will be where you get your refreshment from now one, slave," she said. "Your food will be whatever I decide to give you, if I decide you are worthy of it. In other words, your very survival depends on how pleased I am with your performance."

This scared David. Before all of this, this was a fantasy, something to imagine as a possibility for the future. Sure, the idea of living such an existance was wonderful, but he suddenly realized that he never expected he would actually live a life like this. Here he was, in some mistress's field, about live a life of slavery that he knew he could no escape from. He didn't know whether to be scared or excited. He appeared to be a little and a lot of both.

She reached down and grabbed one of his manacled wrists, pulling him up to his feet again. Quickly, she undid his cuffs and then before he realized what was happening, she was fastening stronger manacles onto his wrists. Once the second one was on him, he pulled it taut and that's when he realized it was connected to the wall of the shed by a short chain. Then she reached down and did the same to his ankles. In seconds, he found himself seated against a scattered bunch of hay with his hands and legs tightly fastened to the wall behind him, leaving him very little room to do much more than to lean sideways in a somewhat lying down position, even though it was slightly painful as he felt like he was being pulled to one side the whole time.

"This is just one of the ways you will sleep at night," she said. "I will come to retrieve you in the morning. If it gets too cold for you at night, then you have the option of dying, but I suggest that you do something to get yourself warm because dying is no longer an option for you unless it is something done to you. You have no right to make such decisions for yourself."

He couldn't believe what she was saying. He also couldn't believe she wasn't going to at least leave him a blanket or pillow. This was inhuman.

"Sweet dreams, slave. Sleep well because tomorrow is going to be a very, very long day."

Then she left the shed, leaving him the shadowed darkness as the last rays of light left the cracks in the walls as there were no windows to show day or night. As he heard her footsteps grow fainter and fainter in the early night, he found himself in near tears, wondering if this wasn't possibly the greatest mistake he had ever made. And to make it worse, he realized this was one mistake he wouldn't be able to rectify; he was stuck in this one as long as his owner desired him to suffer. And from his encounters with Mistress Dominique in the past, he knew her to be a woman who truly enjoyed the suffering of another, so he didn't think he was going to get a chance to be leaving anytime soon.

Soon, the near tears became real until he eventually collapsed from exhaustion, the jet lag and the realization that nothing he could do could change his situation.

Chapter VI

There comes a time when you realize you must face up to your situation and then embrace it or fight against it. In the middle of the night, David found himself extremely uncomfortable; his left arm was starting to get really numb from the pain of having slept on it for a length of time. Moving to his other side, the pain subsided a bit, but the chains made it impossible for him to lie down at this angle, so he remained awake for some time until the pain subsided from his left arm and then tried to sleep that way again. Of course, once the pain had started, there was no way to contain it if put through the same stress. In the end, David didn't get a lot of sleep that first night.

In the morning, a time he was both looking forward to and dreading at the same time, he maneuvered himself into a sitting position with his legs behind him, the chains not giving much more room than he had in that position. It was uncomfortable, and it was cold, but it was also the only way things were going to be. He was beginning to realize that. Of course, the locked chains kind of emphasized that point a bit.

Mistress Cynthia appeared first thing that morning. She entered the hut, took one look at him and then laughed. "I just love the look on a slave's first morning."

She moved around him and then examined the chains. "It looks like you slept a little too well last night," she said. "I guess tonight I'll have to pull them a little tighter. I have to remind you of what you are, slave."

He wanted to protest, to explain that this wasn't what he signed up for. He expected to be treated like a treasured piece of property of Mistress Dominique's. He never expected to be treated like this. This wasn't humane. It wasn't even fun.

"Don't even think about it, slave. The first thing in the morning I want to hear from you is that you are breathing. Anything else is superficial and totally unnecessary. I promise you: make one complaint and it will be the last complaint you will ever be able to make."

He stared back at her with anger in his eyes. This was so unfair. He hadn't asked for this. He agreed to be a slave, not some mule thrown into a shed for the night and then threatened first thing in the morning.

Mistress Cynthia undid the chains on his feet and then put shackles on them, much like the ones he had been wearing on the trip to the shed. Then she removed the manacles from his wrists one by one and then shackled his wrists in front of him, connecting the shackles to the chain that ran from his feet. "On your feet, slave. You don't have time to dawdle." He tried to stand up but collapsed instead. He just didn't have the energy to stand.

Instead of compassion, Mistress Cynthia hit him hard with a riding crop she was holding in her hands. Before she hit him with it, he hadn't even seen it. The slash went across his back, and he quickly forced himself back up to his feet, teetering as he tried to stand straight.

She moved up close to him. For the first time, he could see that she was dressed in a casual jogging suit, something that was obviously comfortable to her rather than the fetish gear he kind of expected to see around the place. Well, this was real, so he should have expected that they weren't going to dress to the whims of their slaves.

She placed her hand softly onto his shoulders and caressed them slowly. "Slave, you obviously don't understand how things work here. I don't care if you don't have the energy or ability to do something. If I tell you to fly, you learn to fly. Is that understood?"

He took a deep breath and then answered. "Yes, Mistress Cynthia."

"Very good," she said. "So follow me."

He hobbled after her, feeling dirty, tired, and very naked. When they reached the outside, he was practically blinded by the morning's sunlight. But he knew better to stop as he followed Mistress Cynthia towards a hill even further than the direction he remembered the main house to be. At least he thought he remembered the main house to be back that way.

Over the next hill was a field of plants, an entire farm from what he could see. It was the kind of sight where you expected to see hundreds of farmhands picking the fruit and vegetables, but as they reached it, he realized there was no one but him and Mistress Cynthia.

Mistress Cynthia motioned out to the field. "You are to start with the berry field. There are baskets at the ends of the field. Begin filling them."

He stared back at her. This was what they wanted him to do? Be a farmer? He was a stockbroker. This was ridiculous.

Mistress Cynthia glared at him for a moment. "Slave, I'm noticing a bit of hesitation in you. Are you going to force me to punish you this early in the morning? I promise you that it won't be anything you enjoy."

He turned quickly and headed for the berry field. He didn't know the first thing about farming, other than the few times he visited his uncle in Oklahoma, but even that was really limited. But he knew better than to question Mistress Cynthia. He didn't know how farming would make him a better slave for Mistress Dominique, but as he started to pick through the field, he realized that that really didn't matter. His ability to make decisions had been taken from him the moment he stepped on that plane. Somehow, he didn't think he would be getting that right back anytime soon.

As he worked, he noticed Mistress Cynthia pull out a recliner chair and stretch herself out on it. She removed her sweats and reclined naked, taking in the sun's rays. As David worked, he glanced back every now and then, just hoping for a glimpse of her, but then after awhile he realized she was watching him, and it was then that he realized even his glances were being monitored. So he forced himself to stop looking and kept working. For hours, he wished it would end, but it never did. Hours after that, he started to realize what true slavery really meant, and he wasn't sure he was totally cut out for it. But to make matters worse, he didn't see any way out of it either.

He took one glance back at Mistress Cynthia and noticed she was staring right at him when he looked. She smiled, but he suspected that smile had nothing to do with a mutual feeling of happiness between the two of them. That beautiful mind of hers obviously harbored other thoughts, and as he continued working hard through the field, that thought worried him. It worried him a lot.

Chapter VII

David had been working for hours; he had no actual grasp of the official passing of time, but he knew he was hot, tired, hungry and he was running out of energy. Every time he looked back to see Mistress Cynthia, he could see her smiling with a bit of satisfaction as she soaked in the sun's rays on the recliner she was laying out on. From time to time, she would sip from a bottle of water, look his way, lick her lips and then go back to laying out on the recliner. It was obvious she was totally oblivious to his discomfort.

Or was that it? Was she so in tuned to his discomfort that that was how she was able to relax so well? If so, this really worried him. He didn't know how long Mistress Dominique intended to keep him under the power of Mistress Cynthia, but he was starting to get really scared.

Had it really been since yesterday afternoon that he last ate? Was his lapping of water in the shed the last bit of water he had consumed? This was totally inhuman. Worse than that: it was totally unfair.

His internal complaints were interrupted by a jolt of pain to his naked back. In surprise, he fell down to the dirt, the chains on his body clanking as he hit hard. With the air knocked out of his lungs, he slowly tried to turn over only to see Mistress Cynthia standing over him with a crop of some sorts in her hands. He didn't know much about whips, other than the fact that they hurt a lot if used on him, and this one seemed like it was designed from some feudal nightmare factory. It was a flogger; he recognized that much, but the ends appeared to be made of metal strips. At least that's what it looked like, and that's certainly what it felt like.

He was sure he was bleeding. He could feel the cool breeze on his back, even though it was a hot day. That breeze was interacting with the open wounds on his freshly cut back.

"Turn over, slave!" she ordered.

He slowly maneuvered himself so that he was lying on his back, facing up to her. The manacles kept his hands in front of his chest, and there was little maneuverability for the rest of his body as the chain connecting all of the wrist, ankle and collar manacles were tightly linked.

He stared up at Mistress Cynthia, not exactly sure what he had done wrong.

Without even addressing him, Mistress Cynthia, kicked his legs apart until they reached the maximum length they could go with the chain still holding them together. From the look on her face, it was obvious that he was not to allow the chain to slacken, that his legs were to be kept as far apart as he could manage. Then she raised the whip and hit him hard on the left leg, halfway between his groin and knee. The pain stabbed through his body. Then she slashed the whip in the same spot again, causing even more pain. Before he could recover from the second blow, she lashed him across the lower leg and then in almost the same swoop movement, hit him in the upper leg portion of his right leg, then following down with two more lashes to the lower leg.

The pain was unbearable. There hadn't even been a warm-up, like Mistress Dominique would always do with him. This was straight out pain.

Then she stood over him, placing her shoe onto his stomach. "Slave, your productivity leaves a lot to be desired."

He couldn't believe what he was hearing. He was dead tired, and he was doing the best he could do.

"If you were an employee, I would have you fired. But you are not an employee. You are a slave. So, you don't get fired. You get punished."

He stared up at her in fear. He didn't know why she was doing this. There was no doubt in his mind that he was doing the very best job he could do. How could he do any better?

She brought the crop down on his groin, at the same intensity as she had done on his legs. He screamed out in pain.

"Slave, perhaps you don't realize the significance of the situation. You have no rights here. I own you completely until I feel that you are worthy of serving your mistress. Until that time, your life is mine. You would do very well to remember that I can do anything I want to you."

She brought down the whip a second time; he screamed even louder than the first time.

She sighed. "Slave, this screaming of yours is getting on my nerves. From this point on, I forbid you to make another sound." She smiled with a touch of innocence crossing her face. "You wouldn't want me to remove any bodily organs on your first day now, would you?"

He couldn't believe she would do something that extreme, but then again, there was no way to know for sure. He never believed they would throw him out into the fields to be a farmer either, and they kept him in chains all night long, and apparently, they were planning to do a lot more than just that. So, he couldn't really be sure.

Mistress Cynthia's hostile expression turned to one that resembled compassion, or what David considered must have been her look of compassion, if she had any. "Slave, you understand that it is you who is making this necessary, don't you? Nothing bothers me more than to have to inflict pain upon someone for failing to perform his duties in a manner worthy of my specifications. I don't want to hurt you, but there's nothing I can do about it. I'm afraid you're causing this all by yourself."

He couldn't believe this. He didn't do anything to cause this.

She hit him in the genitals again; he screamed in shock as well as surprise.

The compassionate expression on her face turned to a look of anger. "I don't believe you just did that. Didn't I just give you a direct order, slave?"

He looked up at her in horror. Yes, she had just told him that under no circumstances was he to make any more sounds. A scream was obviously a sound.

"You know, slave, most slaves who come through here usually live through their first day. I'm starting to wonder about you?"

"I'm so sorry, Mistress Cynthia. It was just so...."

"So _what_, slave? _So_ hard? _So_ intense? A little too much for you now?" She looked up into the sky for a moment and then stared back down at him. "So, let me see if I get this right? You're trying to tell me how hard and how intense your punishment should be. Is that what I'm hearing here?"

He thought quickly. The logic didn't seem to make sense, but he realized he would have to answer her question. "No, Mistress Cynthia."

She laughed. "So, you're calling me a liar then."

His eyes opened wide. He hadn't called her a liar. He knew that. "No, Mistress Cynthia."

She shook her head no. "You know, slave, perhaps you should quit before you end up being castrated out in this field. If you didn't call me a liar, you're stating that I'm mistaken. And if you're not stating that I'm mistaken, then you are stating that I am a liar. Well, slave, what do you have to say about this?"

He didn't know what to say. There was no way out of this. He said nothing.

She laughed even harder than before. "So, you've decided to not answer a direct question, huh? Is that your response?"

Mistress Dominique never played games like this with him. She was strict and stern, but she never goaded him into word games that he couldn't get out of. And he had the strange sensation and feeling that told him Mistress Cynthia wasn't playing any games here.

Mistress Cynthia draped the crop's flexible ends over his groin area and caressed his cock and balls as she moved the crop back and forth, looking up to glance into his eyes from time to time. "I'll let you in on a little secret, slave. I can be a sweet, sensuous mistress if I want to be. But I'll also let you in on a fact of reality here. I'm also an evil bitch who can be quite vicious to the right individual. Already, I've discovered that I don't like you. You're what we call a fuck-up here. You seem to be doing what you're doing for your own desires, not ours, not mine. If you learn anything here by the time I'm done with you, it's that your desires, your fantasies, your every thought process, means nothing to a truly dominant woman. You exist for our pleasure, or for our comfort. Your life here will be filled with horrors, and it will be filled with endless tasks that you might not understand, and they may never be explained to you. You have no rights, no purpose in life other than what we, what I, tell you. You are a worthless animal that has been captured by superior beings, and these beings don't like the animal they found. So, we need to train you, push you into the direction that will make you a better animal. If we never reach that goal, then you will be disposed of as the worthless creature you are. If you do achieve that goal through us, then you will live the rest of your life in our service, in the service of your mistress. Your dreams and goals will come from her. She will transform any thoughts you have into thoughts that benefit her. And don't you ever forget that."

He stared back up at her, not sure of what to say. It was then that he realized she hadn't asked him anything. To speak would have been an insult to her. And that was the last thing in the world he wanted to do, insult Mistress Cynthia.

She smiled. "I hope some of this has filtered into that male mind of yours. I understand that you are not totally capable of grasping all that a woman might tell you, but I do demand that you try your hardest to retain anything I tell you. After all, if the words come from a woman such as me, they should be valued by you as words from Heaven, or possibly above that."

He said nothing.

The smile grew even deeper. "So, slave, where were we?"

Then she lifted the crop, took one sinister look at him, and then started hitting him harder than before. But this time, she didn't stop. At least, not for a very long time after she started.

As David laid on the ground receiving his punishment, he prayed for the pain to stop, for any sign of mercy. But as expected, no one was answering his prayers this afternoon. He was on his own, and there appeared to be very little mercy left in the universe.

Chapter VIII

David didn't know whether to feel relief or dread at the thought that the day was over. After Mistress Cynthia finished beating him yet another time for reasons he still didn't quite understand, she ordered him up onto his feet, told him to clean up the little area where he had been working, place the day's pickings in a cart located at the far end of the field, and then return to where she was.

"So, slave, how was your first day in the fields?"

He so much wanted to tell her that this was not the life for him. He was not a farmer; he was a portfolio manager, and hands-on wasn't something he was very good at. He sort of assumed that Mistress Dominique would have wanted to use him for his economic skills, not menial labor. He so much wanted to tell Mistress Cynthia that this was beneath him. But he realized that sort of response would not be taken too kindly; he also realized it would probably start the beatings all over again.

Now she was marching him back to the area of the shed again, the place where he had spent his first night. How could he tell this evil woman that he didn't want to spend another night chained up to the wall, barely able to reach the ground to sleep. He wanted a bed, a blanket and some kind of comfort. They were treating him like some subhuman, and he felt he deserved so much more.

When they reached the shed, he tried so hard to form the words that would allow him to say what he needed to say. He realized if he didn't say anything else, she was going to lock him to the manacles again and then leave him for another cold night. Oh, God, not another night like that.

"Mistress Cynthia--" he managed after a couple of seconds of reflection, aware of the punishment he might receive for speaking without her permission.

She whirled around and glared at him, her eyes revealing that whatever morsel of information he was about to spew out had better be crucial to the survival of the human species because from the look in her eyes, nothing else seemed to be of importance to her. "What is you want, slave?"

He took a deep breath and let it out before speaking. He was using the time for forming his thoughts, even though he was dead tired from lack of sleep the night before and exhaustion from out in the fields. "Mistress Cynthia, I know it is not my place to say, but must I sleep chained to the wall again this evening?"

She didn't even answer. She just started laughing at him. Then without even addressing the situation, she ordered him to the area behind the shed, the smile still very present on her face.

"Stand up against the wall," she said.

He glanced at the blank shed wall. There were no manacles hanging from it, so if she was going to secure him there, he wasn't sure how it was going to happen. When he turned back to face Mistress Cynthia, she was holding a hose in her hands. There was a pressure nozzle on the end of it.

"Mistress Dominique requires her slaves to be clean at all times. You have been working in the fields all day long, and I don't believe you've had a bath since you arrived here."

He said nothing. He didn't welcome the thought of cold water running all over his body, but he did feel pretty slimey from the work he had done. Still, when he originally thought of a life of slavery, he kind of assumed he would be afforded simple amenities, like a shower. The magazines and hot stories never really seemed to cover the logistics of the situation.

Before he could say anything else, as if he would have anyway, she turned on the water pressure and drenched his front side with the water from the hose. Then she ordered him to turn around and drenched his other side. In seconds, he was totally soaked.

Then, to his surprise, she tossed him a bar of soap and ordered him to lather up his body. Quickly, he did, and then she sprayed him once again. Once done, he was standing before her, dripping all over the grass.

"Into the shed!" she said.

Without hesitation, he walked into the shed and right over to the manacles on the far wall, realizing she was going to lock him away for the night. In total silence, she chained him up and then patted his wet hair with her hand, like an owner to a good puppy. "Slave, you need to realize your station in life here. I've had slaves like you before who believe that their good service to their mistress is what makes them special. You fail to understand what it means to be a slave here. We expect perfect service at all times; anything less would be totally unacceptable. No slave rises above his natural state of submission here because we cannot expect anymore than perfection. But by the same token, we require no less as well."

He pulled on his wrist manacles, realizing they were a bit tighter this evening. He was not relishing the thought of sleeping like this once again. Tears started to fill his eyes again, but before he could lose control, he felt Mistress Cynthia slip a blindfold over his eyes and then he felt her holding him close in her arms, almost like a mother would do to a child. "Hush, slave. This is all for your own good."

He rested quietly in her arms for a few minutes, counting each second as an eternity of bliss as this was the first intimate moment he had received since giving up his pampered life. Then she broke away from him and he could hear her walking to the other side of the shed. Then he heard her walking back and then felt her breath as she was directly in front of him.

"Open your mouth, slave," said Mistress Cynthia.

He did, quickly, but he didn't know what was going to happen. It was then he felt something go into his mouth. It was soft and wet. Instant recognition told him it was lettuce. For the first time in a long time, he remembered that he hadn't eaten in a very long time.

"Chew it slowly, slave. I don't want you getting sick and choking while under my care."

He did as she instructed, and then she fed him yet another piece of this salad. For the next ten or so minutes, he ate what was a very small dinner, but he savoured every bite. When it was finished, he felt Mistress Cynthia pull him into her arms again. "You see, slave, we can be kind to our charges if we so desire. You've already experienced a taste of the horrors that will exist here, but you should understand that slavery means living on both sides of the fence. You just never get to choose which side you're on."

"Thank you, Mistress Cynthia," was all he could think of to say.

"Oh, you're welcome, slave. Now, sleep well. You have an extremely rough day ahead of you tomorrow."

Then she left him in his immobilized darkness to savour her last words and a cool breeze that was moving into to claim the early evening.

Chapter IX

The routine for David over the next couple of days was an early morning wake-up by Mistress Cynthia and then an endless day of working in the fields while Mistress Cynthia relaxed and enjoyed her day in the sun. Over the course of the day, Mistress Cynthia would find reason after reason to beat him, harass him, or just deviously torture him. When the day was over, she would lock him in the shed for the night with so much as a tiny bit of food to sustain him enough for the next day.

This went on for many weeks, and David was starting to get used to the routine, although he longed for anything different. He missed Mistress Dominique, the woman to whom he had offered his entire life and existance to. Instead, every day was met with Mistress Cynthia, a sadist of a woman who took great comfort in his discomfort.

There were days that stretched into the nights when David could see the stars starting to come out in the sky. Before, he was never much of a nature kind of person, or someone who would be interested in the affairs of the stars. But on some of these evenings, he would stare for minutes, while picking fruit and vegetables, of course, but that little break from such horrors of every day living were such tiny salvations that he longed for each tiny moment he could take away from the vicious monotony of such slavery.

One day, after she showered him in the morning, something unusual as she usually drenched him right before the evening meal, she led him back in the direction of the main house. For the first time in weeks, he was no longer going back to the fields in the morning; they were heading to the main house.

He was excited beyond belief. This was the moment he had been waiting for. He had actually started to wonder if it would ever happen again, or if his sole existance in life would be working in the fields. He hated the fields so much, and this seemed so much closer to what he was longing for in life. He was finally going to get to see Mistress Dominique.

He was led through the gazebo entrance and taken into what

had to be best described as a throne room. There was a black leather chair at one end of it with a red carpet stretching from the chair to the other side of the room. David was led to the red carpet by Mistress Cynthia. David's eyes were on the floor, as per Mistress Cynthia's continuous instructions to him, so he didn't even see as Mistress Cynthia addressed someone else, but he certainly heard it. "Mistress Clara, I give you slave David."

"Thank you, Mistress Cynthia. We will call you if necessary."

Then David heard a door open and close, indicating that Mistress Cynthia was now gone. For several minutes, David remained on his knees, staring down at the red carpet, afraid to look up.

"He hasn't looked up once," said another woman's voice. "Mistress Clara, do you think Mistress Cynthia has totally broken him already?"

"Well, Mistress Alicia, we'll just have to see about that."

Then the door opened again, and he heard high heels as they walked slowly across the carpet, passing his view and then stopping as the person sat down on the throne facing him. "You may raise your eyes now, David," she said.

David looked up to see his mistress seated on the throne, a glass of wine in her hands. She wore a black housecoat for comfort, but from the cut of the coat, it was also utilized to drive her slaves and submissives wild with envious desire. David took a deep breath and held his ground.

Mistress Dominique stared back at him. "So, David, have you started to get a hang on how things are here?"

"Yes, Mistress Dominique," he said.

She smiled. "David, I am your owner. You do not need to use my name in your address to me. I am your mistress."

"Yes, Mistress," he said.

"Good," she replied. "Are you and Mistress Cynthia getting along?"

He didn't know how to answer this one.

She stared at him, a puzzled look on her face. "Has she been mistreating you, slave?"

He still said nothing.

"You know, slave, it is totally within my rights to punish you at any time I desire, even if you haven't done anything wrong. So, you would do well to answer your mistress when you are addressed."

"Yes, Mistress. I am sorry. Mistress Cynthia...uh...I think she hates me."

Mistress Dominique just smiled even brighter than before. "Then you are getting along. Good."

It was then that David realized there were two women standing behind him, only several feet away. He didn't look back, but he could sense them back there behind him. He only assumed that they were Mistresses Clara and Alicia.

Mistress Dominique addressed the two women. "Bring him to the massage room. I am in need of one of his massages."

"Yes, Mistress," said one of them as they pounced on David and then dragged him through the doorway into another room. He was still chained with the ankle, wrist, and collar cuffs, but one of them reached down and chained his collar to a hook in the floor using a very long chain. "This is just so you don't get any strange ideas and try to run away, slave."

Then the two of them left and closed the door behind them.

David quickly dropped to his knees. He had no plans of running away, and even as he looked down at the chain and realized there was a lock on it, not just a clasp, he realized it wouldn't have done him much good if he tried.

A couple of minutes later, Mistress Dominique appeared and closed the door behind her. She was wearing that same black, body-cut housecoat and then stripped out of it in front of him. "No massage should ever be given through clothing," she said.

David's eyes opened wide. He'd seen Mistress Dominique naked before; he'd given her several dozen massages in the past; but for some reason seeing her this time made his heart nearly explode.

"David, you're staring."

He dropped his eyes.

She stared to laugh. "David, I'm flattered when you stare, but I worry for you. If you stare long enough, you're not going to be able to do anything I need done, and that won't do either one of us any good."

She stretched herself out face down on the massage table and waited for David to begin. David grabbed the lotion and placed some on his hands, rubbing it evenly, and then he started massaging her back in slow, round circles, pressing slightly and then harder as he rubbed more of the lotion into her skin. He continued until he heard the inevitable moan and then continued on from there.

The massage lasted for several hours, and when he was done, when Mistress Dominique told him he was done, he dropped back down to his knees. She sat up on the side of the massage table and just smiled at him. "I knew there was a reason I took ownership over you."

He said nothing. This was one of those moments where words reallly didn't mean a whole hell of a lot.

She stepped up from the table and moved behind him, caressing his shoulders as she did. "So, how does it feel being truly owned?"

He searched for the right words. "It's different than I expected, Mistress."

She continued caressing his shoulders. "That's usually the way it is with slaves. I didn't think it would be any different for you. Fortunately, I learned from those in the past that giving an option to leave is the same as asking them to leave. Do you find yourself wanting to leave from time to time? Now, be honest."

"Yes, Mistress."

"Then keeping you here is the best thing in the world for you. If I allowed you to leave because you didn't think you could handle it, you'd always regret your decision to leave for the rest of your life. After taking ownership of you, I took away that choice. You can't leave, you can't make that choice."

He thought about it. If she had given him the option to leave, he was sure he would have run at the very first opportunity. He still didn't think he was cut out for this.

"You see, David," she said as she ran her fingers through his hair, "slavery is a continuing series of sacrifices and that's from both sides. You sacrifice every day to serve your mistress. But your mistress sacrifices every day to be your mistress as well. I sacrifice the desire to let you go, to release you so that you don't suffer anymore, but that's one of those sacrifices others never see. David, do you know how much it pains me to see a slave suffering? I can't even begin to describe it. But I sacrifice my motherly desire to let him go, to let you go, because I realize that by staying strong, by being unbending, I am giving us both the opportunity to explore deeper into your very being. Does this make any sense to you, David?"

He thought about it for some time. "I believe so, Mistress."

"You're good, David, even when you don't understand. At least you try." She walked around him and then sat back down on the massage table, facing him. "I use to let you masturbate every other day. How long has it been now?"

It was embarrassing to discuss this, but she was the only woman he felt comfortable discussing such issues. "Mistress Cynthia has not let me do it once."

"It's been seven weeks?" she said, a bit surprised.

Seven weeks? Had he been working in the fields that long? Mistress Cynthia never let him know the date or even the time, so it was very possible. He just knew it had been a very, very long time. "Yes, Mistress."

She reached down and grabbed his hair, pulling him closer to her. "Well, slave, I'm sorry to say that I don't think I would get much out of it right now, so you'll have to wait until I'm in the mood to see you do it."

Disappointment certainly crossed his face.

"Oh, don't be upset, David. It's all part of your new life. You see, you told me a long time ago that you desired a caged environment, a place where I could put you and you would never be able to escape. Think of that as what you are living in." She made a sweeping motion with her free hand. "This whole complex is your cage, and only I hold the key to the cell's door. But that's the way it was meant to be, wasn't it?"

He said nothing.

She grabbed her housecoat, draped it over her arm and then opened the door, turning back to David as she did. "David, thank you for the massage. Mistress Cynthia should be here shortly to take you back to your daily routine."

His eyes opened wide. He thought that part of his training was over. "But, Mistress--"

The smile disappeared from her face. "Don't even try, David. I hold the keys to your cell's door, and right now, I'm locking you right back in." She took in an airy breath and almost swooned as she did it. "Perhaps in another seven weeks you might be ready to move onto the next step. But until then, you have a lot of training left to do."

Then she closed the door after her, leaving David chained to the floor and awaiting a most certain return of Mistress Cynthia.

Chapter X

His first hint of consciousness came to him when it was pitch dark. David Bruester, feeling a chill breeze running across his naked body, went to pull his blanket closer to him, but two things immediately became obvious. One, there was no blanket, and two, his hands were shackled behind him, and there were chains going up and down his body, locking him to the wall behind him. He struggled quickly against the chains, still reeling from a very interesting sensual dream he had just awakened from, although the details of that dream were quickly fading from him as reality blended and canceled out that fantasy world. Then it all came back to him.

He was locked in chains from neck to ankles, and the chains were secured to the wall directly behind him, forcing him to rest on his side with very little room for any maneuverability. Mistress Cynthia, the human version of Satan, had locked him away the night before at least from his impression of her. Well, if Satan were a young, beautiful woman who liked to torture slaves, then it would have been just like that.

It only took him a second to remember what was happening to him. This wasn't exactly what he signed up for when he first signed that contract with Mistress Dominique. As a matter of fact, this was almost completely the opposite of what he was expecting. Like most submissives hoping for a real life slavery situation, he expected that being Mistress Dominique's slave would have been more about a strict household environment under Mistress Dominique's direct control. Instead, what happened when he came to Mistress Dominique's ranch, which its existence came as a complete surprise to him when he was brought there, was he was turned over to a young mistress under Mistress Dominique's tutelage, and David never saw Mistress Dominique again. It did not make a lot of sense to him, and even though this wasn't the environment to demand such a thing as an explanation of justification: it didn't seem very fair either.

That was probably what bothered him the most. It did not seem quite fair. He had signed a contract with Mistress Dominique to be completely owned by her for a period of two years. However, he always assumed that he would be serving her, not someone he never met before the woman's whip first came down upon him. If it weren't for the fact that there did not seem to be an option for escaping this place, he probably would have left when he first arrived.

And that was another problem. He didn't even know when he first arrived. Mistress Cynthia kept him in the barn, chained to the wall every night, and he worked in the fields being some untalented farmer throughout each day, and he was given very little information to help him figure out what was going on beyond the tasks that were given to him by his controller. At some point, in between beatings for not performing to Mistress Cynthia's expectations, he lost complete track of how long he had been in this place.

In addition to that, he appeared to have lost more than his track of time. He lost track of his freedom completely. In the past, before the contract, he served as Mistress Dominique's houseboy, and there was always a strong sense of intimacy between them. She kept telling him over and over that his sufferings at that time were slowly earning him the eventual privilege of being her personal slave, and he worked harder and harder for that day in with an almost quixotic energy. However, when the day finally came, he always assumed that it was going to be a lot more of the same he had already been through with her, but that she would probably push him a little further than she had before. The existence of this ranch two or so hours out from San Francisco was never even a thought on David's mind. Perhaps he should have asked a few more questions before anxiously signing that contract, fearful it would run away from him if he didn't sign it fast enough.

Mistress Dominique was a highly sought after professional dominant, and it was in that capacity that David first met her. At one point, she gave up the business and converted her savings into a very professional business involving worldwide financial transactions that seemed to be very successful for her, mainly run by previous submissives who still managed to do her bidding over the years. To be honest, David really had little idea what it was Mistress Dominique did for a living these days, and his only question he ever asked was whether or not it was legal, and she said that it was, so he never asked another question about it again.

But to a submissive seeking the ultimate domme, this appeared to be the perfect circumstance. Hell, if most submissives knew about the addition of the ranch and its lifestyle, he could have imagined they would be even more interested than they already were. But unfortunately for whomever came in contact with the place, it was one of those revelations that came too late for one to think again. As a matter of fact, the one thing David remembered more than anything else was the barb wire that faced inwards on the fence surrounding the complex, or at least the entrance because he had no clue how large the complex might be, and he also remembered the female guard that was standing at the entrance, smiling when her eyes met with David's, a smile not of friendship or mutual pleasure, but mischievous, knowing far more than David suspected at the time.

David was in a weird sense of hell, a hell that some men and women would have killed to be in while others would have killed to avoid. To this point, David wasn't sure which one he was. But at the same time, it didn't really matter. There was very little choice in the matter for him as it was.

Chapter XI

The arrival of Mistress Cynthia was always something David began to both fear and desire. The fear factor was obvious and completely understandable. The woman was outright mean, and she never held back her punishments for any reason whatsoever. The desire factor was not as easy to understand, but he suspected it had much to do with how beautiful she was, and the way she tended to tease him, making him think that she punished him because it benefited him in the long run and really wished she didn't have do to so. It only took a second for him to realize that she loved punishing him more than anything, and she just happened to be the greatest actress to come across his way in years.

The routine for David over this span of time was an early morning wake-up by Mistress Cynthia, quite often a surprise wake-up and continuous yelling, slapping and hits with a riding crop until he was completely ready to her standards of what "being ready" really meant. And that seemed to change with each morning, so no matter how hard he tried, he never seemed to get on the better side of her in the morning. There was always something wrong: not moving fast enough, didn't stand erect enough for her, hard-on without permission (yes, that was always a fallback one for her cause it never failed to happen once she started yelling at him), and a every now and then something that seemed to translate as "you men think you can get away with everything", indicating that he was probably being punished for something some other guy had done to her recently or some time in the past.

Then he be hurried to the fields where Mistress Cynthia would relax on one of the recliners that she would order him to retrieve for her, taking him away from his work for a moment to make sure that she was comfortable, and then she would yell at him for taking so long to get back to work, that this wasn't some freeloading job he was doing here. For most of the day, David would pick whatever fruit or vegetable that Mistress Cynthia would require of him. Sometimes, she would begin such a day by stating something along the lines of "I really crave apples today" and then would say nothing else, leaving him trying to figure out if apples even grew anywhere out in this vast wilderness that was owned by Mistress Dominique. A few times, Mistress Cynthia punished him harshly for not finding an item she desired. Once, it was a vegetable she named that he never heard of, so he spent the entire day bringing back samples of different vegetables he didn't recognize in hopes that he had the right one for her. On that day, he often wondered if the vegetable was made up on the spot by Mistress Cynthia, because he never managed to find it, and at the end of the day, she pulled him by the ear to a bush and pulled a sample from it, stating this was the one. And even though he could not say anything about it, he really suspected that he had visited that tree and presented her with the same vegetable a few times that same day, but he was not allowed to ever make such a statement. Another time, she had him searching out a certain fruit, and after only a few hours, he came to believe that perhaps this fruit didn't even grow in this particular hemisphere. But if it did not, that was probably his fault, and Mistress Cynthia made sure he remembered that.

Over the days, Mistress Cynthia would find any reason to beat him, harass him, or just deviously torture him. When the day was over, she would lock him in the shed for the night with so much as a tiny bit of food to sustain him for the next day. David was never much of a "salad guy", but during his weeks with Mistress Cynthia, he certainly began to savor the taste of lettuce, a very common meal she fed him before putting him to bed for the night. When one subsists on very little, that little becomes very attractive.

This went on for many weeks, and David was beginning to get used to the routine, although he longed for anything different. And then he began to question that desire, because every time that Mistress Cynthia presented something different, it was never anything he came to like better than what happened before. He complained once that the straw she had him sleep on was very uncomfortable, so she had him remove it and then made him sleep on the hard floor of the barn. It took several days of begging from him to get her to acquiesce and give him back his straw. That pretty much sums up how it was like with Mistress Cynthia.

He missed Mistress Dominique, the woman to whom he pledged his life and existence. He had desired the pleasure of being her slave for many years, and she knew that. When she finally offered him that position, after filtering out many other men who were trying for that same privilege, he felt he had achieved the greatest position anyone could ever achieve. He wanted to put out a memo at work and let everyone know, but it only took him a few seconds to realize how much of mistake that would have been. However, he took great pleasure in quitting that job and turning over his life to his future mistress. Unfortunately, that life he expected after becoming her slave didn't materialize. Instead, every day was met with the very cruel Mistress Cynthia, a sadist of a woman who took great comfort in his discomfort. Sometimes he wondered if she went home after she chained him up for the night or if she just stuck around for the night, waiting to see if he might make a mistake in his sleep cycle and then punish him again. As this had not happened yet, he assumed this was not the case because if she had been around, she most definitely would have found a reason to punish him for sleeping wrong.

That is not to say that there were not pockets of pleasure in David's days. Yes, it was a horrible experience for someone to have to go through, but sometimes when he was working the fields, the days would stretch into nights, and Mistress Cynthia left him to continue working, and then David could watch as the stars started to come out in the sky. Before, he was never much of a nature person, or someone who would be interested in the affairs of the stars. But on some of these evenings, he would stare for minutes, while picking fruit and vegetables, of course, but that little break from such horrors of his everyday life were such tiny salvations that he longed for each tiny moment he could take away from the vicious monotony of such slavery.

And there were pockets of pleasure from none other than Mistress Cynthia herself. As surprising as it may seem, there were times when the demoness from Hell would approach him with kindness and a sense of sensual sensitivity, rubbing his shoulders after a long bout of work and offering him positive reinforcement verbally for a job well done. Those moments were rare, but they seemed to be the only thing he could truly strive for, and when they happened, it seemed to make everything horrible disappear for a moment of time.

One morning, after she ordered him to be ready for yet another day, she led him to the place where she normally hosed him down and then did just that. This was unusual as she normally showered him before his evening meal and then would put him to bed. So this threw off the usual procedure she instituted for each day.

Then she led him out of the barn and marched him in his hobbling chains in the direction of the main house. For the first time in weeks, he was not being led back to the fields first thing in the morning; instead, they were heading towards the main house.

He was excited beyond belief, although there was a slight sense of apprehension as Mistress Cynthia was not beyond playing little games with him to make him think something good was happening when in reality it was not. Yet, he believed that this was the moment he had been waiting for. He had actually started to wonder if it was ever going to happen again, of if he was going to live the rest of his life working in the fields for Mistress Cynthia and her daily desires of particular food items. He hated the fields so much, and this seemed so much closer to what he was longing for in life. He was finally going to get to see Mistress Dominique.

Mistress Cynthia led him through the gazebo entrance and pushed him into what would best be described as a throne room. There was a black leather chair at one end of it with a red carpet stretching from the chair to the other side of the room. Mistress Cynthia led David to the red carpet. David's eyes were on the floor, a reflection of Mistress Cynthia's continuous instructions to him, so he didn't see what was going on as Mistress Cynthia addressed someone else in the room, but he certainly heard the exchange. "Mistress Clara, I give you slave David."

"Thank you, Mistress Cynthia. We will call you if necessary."

David started to wonder if he was being turned over to yet another mistress. Then he heard a door open and close, indicating that Mistress Cynthia was gone. For several minutes, David remained on his knees, naked, in chains, wanting so much to look up but fearing the consequences of such a brash action.

"He hasn't looked up once," said another woman's voice. "Mistress Clara, do you think Mistress Cynthia has totally broken him already?"

"Well, Mistress Alicia, we'll just have to see about that."

One of the women, which one was totally unknown to David as he had not yet had enough experience with them to know which woman was which, stepped over to him and ran her fingers across his back with a very caressing touch, not harsh like he came to expect from Mistress Cynthia. Then the door opened again, and she stopped, and he could feel her body heat as it dissipated, indicating she was moving further away from him.

The sound of high heels could be heard walking slowly across the carpet, making a distinct sound slightly muffled by the cushioning of the carpet itself. He heard the sound of those high heels as they moved near him and then continued on past him, stopping as the person sat down on the throne facing him. "You may raise your eyes now, David," she said.

David looked up to see Mistress Dominique staring back at him. She, like always, was the most beautiful woman he had ever known, and she only appeared even more beautiful to him as he took in the sight of the woman for whom he was suffering. She wore a black housecoat that she wore for comfort, but it was one of those housecoats designed by a very expensive label that knew exactly how to accentuate the look of a beautiful woman. It had slits up the sides of the legs that appeared to go all the way up to the top of the garment and the cut of the housecoat appeared designed with the sole purpose of driving slaves insane and wild with envious desire. David took a deep breath and made no attempt to do anything other than what his mistress would order of him.

Mistress Dominique stared into his eyes for a moment and then looked him up and down. "Sit up, slave, so that I may see my property properly."

He maneuvered himself into a crouching position that was more to her expectations. Her eyes roamed across his body and then stopped at his manhood. Her reaction surprised him. It was a smile. "I see some things haven't changed."

He was completely hard. There was no hiding that.

Mistress Dominique turned her attention back to eye contact. "So, David, have you started to get a hang of how things are done here?"

"Yes, Mistress Dominique," he said.

She smiled again. "David, I am your owner. You do not need to use my name in your address to me. I am your mistress. All others require titles because they do not mean to you what I mean to you."

"Yes, Mistress," he said.

"Good," she replied. "Are you and Mistress Cynthia getting along?"

He didn't know how to answer that one.

She stared at him, a puzzled look on her face. "Has she been mistreating you, slave?"

He still said nothing. This was one of those areas where he

didn't know what was expected of him. Was what Mistress Cynthia was doing to him really "mistreating" him or was it what he should have been expecting? How do you answer something like that to a woman who takes pleasure in torturing you?

"You know, slave, it is totally within my rights to punish you at any time I desire, even if you haven't done anything wrong. So, you would do well to answer your mistress when you are asked a question by her."

"Yes, Mistress. I am sorry. Mistress Cynthia…uh…I think she hates me."

Mistress Dominique just smiled even brighter than before. "Then you are getting along well. Good."

It was then that David realized there were still two women standing behind him, only several feet away. He didn't look back, but he could sense them back there behind him. He assumed they were Mistress Clara and Alicia. A strange thought went through his mind as he wondered why Mistress Dominique required guards with her personal slave kneeling before her. Was it possible that past experience had made such a presence necessary, that there was some fear that an enslaved, tortured being might strike out at his mistress in some attempt at vengeance and escape?

Mistress Dominique addressed the two women. "Bring him to the massage room. I wish to take advantage of the one thing I know he does well."

"Yes, Mistress," said one of them as they pounced on David and dragged him through the doorway into another room. It happened so fast and so violently that David was completely taken by surprise by the action. He was still chained with the ankle, wrist and collar manacles, but one of them reached down and chained his collar to a hook in the floor using a very long chain. "This is just so you don't get any strange ideas and try to run away, slave."

The other one started laughing and said to her partner: "Remember the guy that got away and had us chasing him through the halls."

She nodded. "I don't think he expected the response he received at his trial." She shook her head. "A perfect example of how stupid men really are. One of these days you and I should visit the prison and see how he's doing these days."

"Not sure if I want to. I hate that place. Those girls that run that place are a little too mean for my tastes."

"Nothing wrong with loving your work," she said with a smile. Then the two of them left and closed the door behind them.

David quickly dropped to his knees. He had no plans of running away, and even as he looked down at the chain and realized there was a lock on it, not just a clasp, he realized it wouldn't have done him much good if he tried. And he had a strong feeling that the two mistresses weren't just making up stories to scare him either. Something about this place told him that the women here were far more serious than he cared to test.

A couple of minutes later, Mistress Dominique appeared and closed the door behind her. She was wearing that same black, body-cut housecoat and then stripped out of it to nothing in front of him. "No massage should ever be given through clothing," she said.

David's eyes opened wide. He'd seen Mistress Dominique naked more times than he could count; he'd given her tons of massages in the past; but for some reason seeing her this time made his heard nearly explode.

Her face turned serious. "David, you're staring."

He dropped his eyes.

She laughed. "David, I'm flattered when you stare, so I don't mind, but I also worry for you. If you stare long enough, you're not going to be able to do anything I need done, and that won't do either one of us any good."

She stretched herself out face down on the massage table and waited for David to begin. David grabbed the lotion and placed some on his hands, rubbing it evenly, and then he started massaging her back in slow, round circles, pressing slightly and then harder as he rubbed more and more of the lotion into her skin. He continued until he heard the inevitable moan and the continued on from there. He knew her body extremely well, and he knew how to please her with a massage, and for the first time since arriving here, he actually felt like he was doing something right.

The massage lasted for several hours, and when he was done, when Mistress Dominique told him he was done, he dropped back down to his knees. She sat up on the side of the massage table and just smiled at him. "I knew there was a reason I took ownership over you."

He said nothing. This was one of those moments where words really didn't mean a whole hell of a lot.

She stepped up from the table and moved behind him, caressing his shoulders as she did. "So, how does it feel being truly owned?"

He searched for the right words, making sure not to take too much time, which would certainly be reasoning for punishment. "It's different than I expected, Mistress."

She continued caressing his shoulders. "That's usually the way it is with slaves. I didn't think it would be any different for you either. Fortunately, I learned from failures in the past that giving an option to leave is the same as asking a slave to leave. Do you find yourself wanting to leave from time to time? Now, be honest."

"Yes, Mistress."

"I thought so. Then keeping you here is the best thing in the world for you. If I allowed you to leave because you didn't think you could handle it, you'd always regret your decision to leave for the rest of your life. I'm not going to let that happen to you. After I took ownership of you, I took away that choice for you. You can't leave, you can't make that choice."

He thought about it. If she had given him the option to leave, he was sure he would have run at the very first opportunity. He still didn't think he was cut out for this.

"You see, David," she said as she ran her fingers through his hair, "slavery is a continuing series of sacrifices and that's from both sides. You sacrifice every day to serve your mistress. But your mistress sacrifices every day to be your mistress as well. I sacrifice the desire to let you go when things get too difficult for you, to release you so that you don't suffer anymore, but that's one of those sacrifices you will never see. David, do you know how much it pains me to see you a slaver suffering? To see you suffering? I can't even begin to describe it. But I sacrifice my motherly desire to let him go, to let you go, because I realize that by staying strong for both of us, by being unbending, I am giving us both the opportunity to explore deeper into your very being. Does this make any sense to you, David?"

He thought about it for some time. "I believe so, Mistress."

"You're good, David, even when you don't understand. At least you try." She walked around him and then sat back down on the massage table, facing him. Her bare foot rested on his left leg and then started moving up until she was running her toes across the length of his very hard cock. She ran it up and down a few times before lifting her foot up off of him, hovering it some distance away from him as she leaned back on the massage table. "I use to let you masturbate once every other day." She ran her foot across his cock again. "How long has it been now?"

It was embarrassing to discuss this, but this was the only woman with whom he felt comfortable discussing such an issue. And she was driving him nuts with her foot. "Mistress Cynthia has not let me do it once."

"It's been seven weeks?" she said, a bit surprised.

Seven weeks? Had he been working in the fields that long? Mistress Cynthia never let him know the date or even the time, so it was very possible. He just knew it had been a very, very long time. "Yes, Mistress."

She ran her foot against his cock a few more times and then retracted it. She then reached down and grabbed his hair, pulling it closer to her. "Well, slave, I'm sorry to inform you that I don't think it I would get much pleasure out of it right now, so you're going to have to wait until I'm in the mood to see you do it."

Disappointment registered all over his face.

"Oh, don't be upset, David. It's all part of your new life. You see, you told me a long time ago that you desired a caged environment, a place where I could put you, use you for my own desires, and you would never be able to escape. You asked to be owned, to have no choice over anything. Think of that as what you are living in now." She made a sweeping motion with her free hand. "This whole complex is your cage, and only I hold the key to your cell's door. But isn't that the way it was meant to be?"

He said nothing.

She grabbed her housecoat, draped it over her arm and then opened the door, turning back to David as she did. "David, thank you for the massage. Mistress Cynthia should be here shortly to take you back to your daily routine."

His eyes opened wide. He thought that part of his training was finally over. "But, Mistress—"

The smile disappeared from her face. "Don't even try, David. I hold the keys to your cell's door, and right now, I'm locking you right back in." She took in an airy breath and almost swooned as she did it, the smile coming back to her face in what looked more like sensual pleasure than an expression of humor. "Perhaps in another seven weeks you might be ready to move onto the next step. But until then, you have al of training left to do. Do not disappoint me, or you will most certainly regret it."

Then she closed the door after her, leaving David chained to the floor and awaiting a most certain return of Mistress Cynthia.

Chapter XII

In most western societies, the movement of night into day is usually welcomed by the masses as a good thing, often as night is equated with dark, and thus, evil, while daylight is equated with light, and thus, good. Horror stories usually take advantage of this state of acceptance, often utilizing the dark to initiate horrific scenes of danger where monsters jump out of the night and cause the audience to jump up in unexpected fear. For most audiences, the dark is to be feared, and the light is to be welcomed with open arms.

That was not the way of the world for David. For him, the dark that came with night was the one moment of the day that offered him respite from the horrors that appeared to come at him during the day. While most of society fears the unexpected actions of the night, David embraced the solitude of knowing that at least at night, he was safe from the horrors of the day. Often, he would stay awake for an hour or so just relishing the moments of uneventful bliss that appeared during this time. For, when daylight appeared, he was guaranteed certain horror that would not come as a surprise, horror that had no escape. So he gladly welcomed the solitude of night.

But David did not fear phantoms or goblins or monsters under the bed. No, the monsters he feared were the human type, and it was just one, one that never failed to appear once daylight began to creep into the barn David considered his nighttime refuge. That monster that appeared was one to be feared, and David had enough experience with that creature to know that there was no escaping its fangs no matter what one did to avoid it.

To see David this evening, one would wonder how one could possibly fear the day when the night appeared to be horrific by its own merits. Unlike most of the populous that existed miles from the place where David was sleeping in this barn, comfort ability was not one of the creature aspects afforded to him. His bed consisted of hay that had been thrown onto the floor of the rickety barn. There was no blanket, pillow or any other sign of comfort to enhance his nightly condition. Even the freedom of maneuverability was a thing of the past for David as his wrists were chained behind him, attached to a heavy set of chains that ran down to a tight locking device around his chest all the way down to locking manacles on his ankles. The chains were pulled tight so that he was forced into a slumped position, and he slept on his side, barely able to move because the swivel part of the chain that extended from his waist piece was attached to a d-ring on the wall next to the hay, keeping him from moving at all. It was very uncomfortable, but escaping such a predicament was not an option for him. This was how his life had been for the many weeks that he had been here.

This was the way he lived for the first seven weeks after arriving at Mistress Dominique's ranch, located two hours in an unknown direction from the hub of San Francisco. During the limousine ride from the airport, the windows had been blackened to David's sight, so he had not given it much thought as the trip had taken so long, and he was tormented by a young woman to whom he had practically forgot everything about her aside from her threats and the soft scent of her beautiful feet to which he had massaged for nearly the entire length of the trip, never quite succeeding at achieving her expectations.

Upon arriving at the ranch, Mistress Dominique, his contracted owner, turned him over to Mistress Cynthia, a young, beautiful, and very strict dominatrix who took great pleasure in making David's life miserable. She put him to work in the fields, picking fruit and performing all sorts of other farm-related duties, something not familiar to a man who had just quit his life as a stockbroker at one of the better-known companies in California. She was cruel and mean, and she rarely missed an opportunity to punish David upon taking charge him after being given license to do so by Mistress Dominique, the owner of this complex that seemed to be much more extensive than David ever imagined possible.

For most of the time on the ranch, David was kept naked, and he was punished for any type of infraction that Mistress Cynthia might levy against him. It was in the seventh week that he was presented to Mistress Dominique once again who acknowledged his training but then sent him back to Mistress Cynthia to continue transforming his life. That fateful night ended with Mistress Cynthia locking him away in the barn for what appeared to be an eternity as the experience of this type of slavery ever seemed to end.

When David woke up that next morning, he expected the usual unlocking of the chains, a standard whipping, spanking, beating or combination of the three and then dragged to the fields and put to work for the day. If he were lucky, he would get a few slices of lettuce in the afternoon sometime; if he were not lucky, then he would be beaten instead. It was not always the best of times for a slave being the property of Mistress Dominique.

However, when Mistress Cynthia came for him that morning, she did not beat him. Instead, she unlocked his chains, attached a chain to his leather collar and then let him hobbling in his chains down a weeded-over path that seemed to lead out to the middle of nowhere. She walked with him hobbling behind her for a very long time, so long that she had to stop a couple of times and take a break. She would drop him to his knees with a brutal lash from her crop, or she would quickly point her finger to the ground and punish him if he didn't take the hint quick enough to satisfy her desire to have all things work as planned in her universe. Then she would drink from her canteen, lick her lips and then put her water away. She would stare at him for a long time with the canteen in her hands, as if she was debating whether or not to offer him a drink, and in the end, every time, she would put the canteen away and order him back to his feet to continue their journey.

But David had no clue where they were going. This trip was out of the ordinary for them. For seven weeks, she had housed him in the same spot, beat him in the same spots, and had him work the same fields. Nothing ever changed, aside from her levels of hostility towards him. Not surprisingly, after having experienced her control for nearly two months, that hostility grew stronger each and every day.

As he walked, David began to wonder how large this ranch was. He knew of a number of estates near the San Francisco area that were large, but this was something he'd never heard of. It had to be the largest, most secluded spot in all of California. Yet, he had no idea where this place might be. How many others had been subjected to this place, and yet as much knowledge as he had concerning the BDSM scene, he'd never heard anything about this place. Even being Mistress Dominique's houseboy for a number of years, at her home in the city, he never even suspected a place like this might exist.

He stopped walking as he realized that Mistress Cynthia had stopped and was staring at him. He readied himself for a whipping or beating that was certain to come.

"Why are you flinching?" she said, in an almost schoolgirl tone of voice. That was definitely a voice he learned to fear from her. It usually meant she was humored and was about to unleash the hounds of hell for the hell of it.

He lowered his head as was expected of him. "I am sorry, Mistress Cynthia."

She pointed to the ground, and he immediately dropped to his knees and kept his eyes down, staring at her black, leather hiking boots and immediately started to wonder where someone would find such a cool thing, something that served both fetish and practical purposes.

"What are you thinking?"

He knew better than to hold anything back. "Mistress Cynthia, I apologize. I was just wondering where someone of your stature actually acquired boots like the ones that you are wearing."

She did what he didn't expect. She smiled. "You're chained up like some galley slave in some ancient Empire, or really bad fantasy movie with Arnold Schwarzeneger before he actually started making movies where you could understand what he was saying. You're being led naked miles into the wilderness for goddess knows what purpose, although experience has already taught you that it won't be for something enjoyable. You're tortured for thinking and then tortured for not thinking at a moment's whim. You walk around with a petrified hard-on for hours upon hour and not once have you been allowed to cum, yet the only question going through your mind is where did I buy my boots?"

It sounded pretty silly to him as well. "Yes, Mistress Cynthia."

She just started laughing. "Well, none of your business, but I have to admit that you surprised me on this one." She continued laughing and then turned and continued walking. Realizing the joke was over, David stood up and continued after her.

The journey lasted hours. David couldn't figure out how many, but the day had started cool, as most early mornings do, and the sun had already been way overhead for quite some time before the thought of time came to mind. Before he could actually ponder further on it, they walked over a hill and then it appeared.

It was a house in the middle of nowhere. Not a barn. Not some shack, but a very nice looking house, the kind you see when walking onto some plantation in the middle of Georgia. Only, this wasn't Georgia, and for the most part, there were no plantations in California. Well, not officially at least.

"We're here," said Mistress Cynthia.

David didn't know what to say, which was a good thing because Mistress Cynthia hadn't given him permission to say anything anyway. He just knew that something about that house didn't make him happy to see civilization again.

They walked until they came close enough for David to realize that it appeared to be lived-in, although there did not appear to be people around who were living in it. "Welcome to your new home, slave," she said as she walked up the stairway to the porch and stopped at the front door.

Well, this was definitely an improvement over the barn, but still David did not feel that his style of living was about to get any better with the house than it was just last night. He climbed the stairs behind Mistress Cynthia, having to hop the stairs one at a time because the chain between his ankles did not give him enough room to actually take one step at a time with each foot. When he reached the top of the porch, he took a quick look around and admired the southern feel to the house, including the Victorian porch swing that seemed to accentuate the place just perfectly.

Mistress Cynthia just stood before the screen door and stared at David. That was when David realized what was wrong. She was waiting for him to open the door for her.

Quickly, he hobbled over and pulled open the screen door, and then he pushed open the main door for Mistress Cynthia. She glared at him for a second, huffed to herself and then walked into the building.

The inside of the house was exactly as David would have expected it. It was like walking onto an indoor set of some well-financed and well-researched Civil War film. Everything seemed to fit the decorum of the place, and it was obvious that a lot of care, and a lot of money had gone into this house.

"It's beautiful, isn't it?" she said.

"Yes, Mistress Cynthia."

She turned to face him and pointed to the floor to which made him immediately drop to his knees. "This is where we are going to be living for some time until I believe you are ready for the next step in your education. This house may appear to be quite beautiful, and I agree that it is, but I promise you that within a few days you are going to grow to hate this house with every ounce of your being. You need to discover that quite often beauty hides cruelty."

David's mind flashed the image of Mistress Cynthia before him. He didn't need to be told that beauty hides cruelty; Mistress Cynthia was the epitome of just that.

A smile came to Mistress Cynthia's face. "God, you are so predictable. Well, slave, let me just tell you that up until now you've only experienced the kind and gentle side of Mistress Cynthia. Prepare to experience true fear." Then she walked out of the room and left him sitting on his knees, waiting to find out what was going to happen in this new place.

Chapter XIII

For some reason, David actually thought there would be some sort of rest break before his training started up again, but that was not to be the case. As it was getting late, he figured that she would have probably put him to bed and then he would be left for the night to ponder the horrors this place might have to offer. Instead, Mistress Cynthia left him on his knees in the main room (what those living in such a place would call The Receiving Room) and wandered off deeper into the house for some time. David knew better than to make a sound, a move or a decision during a time like this.

David hated times like these because it constantly forced him to rethink his decision to come here in the first place. More and more, the time alone caused him to reflect on what a mistake he believed that decision to be. The whole concept of living a life of slavery is a great idea if one is into that sort of thing, but it is almost always a fantasy. David was involved in a number of fetish organizations over the years that always seemed to have humorous stories about submissives seeking out this type of life as a personal lifestyle but would run as far away as possible once that lifestyle was made reality. This was where he was at this time. He knew he wanted the lifestyle. He craved the lifestyle. But now that he had it, he wanted to be anywhere but in this kind of lifestyle.

The fantasies he used to have about being put through a living hell by dominant women used to fuel his imagination for years. He acted upon a number of these fantasies in controlled situations that always seemed to have a designated ending, from professional dominants to the ever-lucky privilege of playing this way with dominant girlfriends. Yet, as much as he fantasized about these situations going beyond the time set for them to end, he never imagined that it would be so difficult once the parameters were no longer a factor or possibility.

"Penny for your thoughts," said the only voice he'd come to know after nearly two months of slavery.

He looked up to see Mistress Cynthia standing in front of him, dressed in a sunflower dress, her hair flowing down freely and a set of vinyl white boots on her feet. It was kind of like looking at a skewed

Southern belle. "Mistress Cynthia, I was thinking about how this would not have been something I would have done if I had known how it was going to lead."

She nodded. "At least you're being honest, slave." She turned around. "Zip me up."

He stood up and took the zipper of her dress and ran it up its track to her neck. It was strange, but for a moment, he felt that this was a huge moment for them, as she never required such a service from him. She was utilizing him for something very personal. And then common sense hit him. This was a freaking zipper. It wasn't like she just decided to have a child with him.

"Follow me," she said as she moved towards the far door.

Quickly, he stepped in behind her and did everything he could to take in the sights of the next room they entered while still trying to pretend that he was only paying attention to her, something he knew she would reinforce if she suspected he was doing anything to the contrary.

The next room was actually the kitchen, a huge one, too. It was stocked with practically everything, indicating that this house was quite in use, even though there did not appear to be any individuals using it other than them at the moment. The knick knacks throughout the kitchen, little wooden carve-out people, potpourri artwork and kitchen utensils and paraphernalia of all types, gave the place a romantic feel to it, but David had a very hard time imagining that anything he was going to experience in the next two years was going to be something he might mistake with romance.

She stopped and walked over to a corner of the kitchen and then reached up to a small rope hanging from the ceiling. For a second, David thought she was going to tie him to it for some type of torturous situation, but instead she pulled the rope and a stairway descended from the upper level to where they were. It was not a bondage rope; it was a rope to bring down the stairs from the next level.

She walked up the stairway, and David made his way to follow behind her, immediately taking in a whiff of dust. While the rest of the place appeared quite immaculate, the area Mistress Cynthia had just opened up wreaked of dust and uncleanliness.

Once up the stairs, David found himself in what had to be some storage area for the house because it was nothing but junk. And it was all over the place, too. The dust was completely out of control here, and David had a bad feeling that he was going to be spending a lot of time here.

Mistress Cynthia pointed to a corner of the room, a room that appeared to be a lower level attic, indicating that there was probably yet another level to this place as well. "You have two hours. I want that area spotless."

He just stared at her.

"Did I stutter?" she said.

"No, Mistress Cynthia. It just doesn't seem possible."

She shook her head. "Well, if you value your hide, it better be possible." Mistress Cynthia walked over to David, inserted a key into the shackles holding his wrists together and then freed his hands, although his manacles were still on his wrists, but not attached to each other. She then turned back to the stairway and started to descend before stopping and speaking again. "Spotless, remember." She then closed the stairway from below and the room turned darker without the light.

David just stared at the shadow of the corner and wondered if it was just dust and junk in that corner.

David did his best to clean the place. He was not much of a maid, but he had much experience as a houseboy for Mistress Dominique, and a stint of service in the Army helped him get beyond the anally retentive drill sergeant that always seemed to find dust where there was cleanliness, but this just did not seem the same. For one thing, in all of those other circumstances, he remembered cleaning something that was relatively clean in the first place. Sure, there might be a bit more dust than expected, but the spots were rarely disgustingly dirty. He didn't even know if there was a trash can on this level, and he certainly did not see any trash bags he could use to store what might not seem to belong.

And what did belong? He couldn't tell the difference between junk and storage clutter. After awhile, realizing that Mistress Cynthia wasn't going to return and then understand his dilemma, he decided to just start separating what he considered to be junk and what he considered to be salvageable.

Hours went by.

When Mistress Cynthia returned, David was not exactly proud

of the job that he had done, but he felt confident that he did the best job he possibly could. There were stacks of stuff away from the corner where he was working, and the corner itself was as spotless as David could make it, made even cleaner with an old dusty mop that he found in one of the other corners of the room. It was not perfect, not as it could have been if he had the appropriate materials to make it so, but he felt confident that he could not have done a better job than he had done.

Mistress Cynthia turned and glared at him for a second, and David immediately dropped to his knees. He knew better than to have to wait for her to tell him to do so. So, he remained silent as she wandered around him, circling him over and over as she glanced around the room. "The corner is clean," was the only thing she said for a long time.

That was a pretty ambiguous comment under the circumstances. Yes, the corner was clean, but that did not exactly mean that she was pleased. Yet, he could do nothing but wait for her to continue which she did after a few minutes of just walking around him over and over again.

"I notice you made three piles of stuff," she said. "Explain yourself."

David thought quickly while trying to remember why he did so. "Mistress Cynthia, one pile was for stuff that was obviously trash, one pile was for items that I found to be questionable, and one pile appeared to be items that I expected would want to be kept."

She examined the three piles. She stopped at the trash pile. "None of this stuff I would have kept." David figured that was some sort of validation or acceptance of his actions. She walked over to the pile of stuff that he expected she would have wanted kept. "Valuable items. Yes, I could see them needing to be kept." Then she walked to the middle pile. She reached down and picked up a toy, something David recognized as a backscratcher. "Why this?"

"Mistress Cynthia, I was not sure whether or not you would want that kept."

"Why not?"

"Mistress Cynthia, if your back was itching, I figured you would want the backscratcher."

She turned and stared at David. "Then why is it not in the valuable items pile?"

He thought quickly, trying to remember why he chose the pile that he did. "As you are a dominant woman, I was not sure if you would think it was a waste as long as there were submissives willing to scratch your back for you."

She tossed the backscratcher onto the trash pile. "Makes sense."

David waited for the shoe to drop, or the anvil, or whatever huge implement she was going to wield against him. But it never came.

"Back to the kitchen," she said.

He rushed down the stairway and then immediately dropped to his knees once on the kitchen floor, but only after making sure he moved out of the way so he did not block Mistress Cynthia. Years ago, when first serving Mistress Dominique, he made a similar blunder, blocking off his mistress in his zest to serve her properly, and needless to say, the rest of the evening was not one where he was rewarded for his desire to serve her properly.

Mistress Cynthia walked over to David and then grabbed his right wrist, forcing it behind his back. A quick jerking motion to his left wrist forced his arms behind his back, and then he heard her snapping the lock on his manacles, forcing him to keep his hands locked behind his back. David really expected it eventually, so it was not much of a surprise, however, he was taken aback when he realized she wasn't finished, feeling something coming over his head and then over his eyes. For the first time in a long time, he found himself blindfolded.

"You are to follow my voice, slave. Do you understand?"

"Yes, Mistress Cynthia," he said, a bit scared although why he wasn't sure. This was an environment where he realized he needed to be scared all the time, not just when blindfolded.

"Follow me," she said, and he could already hear her voice trailing as she started walking. He stood up and started following behind her, bumping into the corner of a counter and then a can on the floor.

A second later, he felt the heat of Mistress Cynthia as she came up really close to him. She then began to move slowly, and he found himself able to follow behind her. At one point, he heard the sound of a door opening, and then he felt a jerk in his neck as she ran her fingers into the ring of his collar and began leading him by pulling on his collar. They started going up stairs. A lot of stairs. Then they turned a corner and continued going up more stairs. Then they walked down a hallway, a very long hallway, and then they were going up more stairs again. A corner and more stairs. David began to get a bit dizzy just from the fact that he had no real center of balance this way other than the fingers locked on the ring of his collar.

At the top of the next level, he was pulled down a long, carpeted walkway and then he heard the sound of a door opening. He stepped through behind Mistress Cynthia, and then he heard the sound of the door closing. He had no clue where he was in the house.

He wanted to ask a question, but he knew that was not a wise thing to do, so he stood silently as Mistress Cynthia unlocked the shackles behind his back. He figured she was going to remove the blindfold, but instead, she turned him around to face her in what was the opposite direction he had been facing, and then she pushed him backwards. His legs buckled and he fell backwards, only realizing right then that she had pushed him onto a bed. She then grabbed his legs, swirled his body 90 degrees so that he was most likely lying down lengthwise on the bed, and then he felt an immediate jolt of pain as she leaped on top of him and straddled his chest on the bed.

For a second, David actually thought she was going to be doing the unthinkable, and he was excited beyond belief, and then he felt his left wrist cupped in her hand and stretched to a corner of the bed. A clasping sound told him that this wrist was now secured, and then the same thing happened to his right wrist. Moving down his body, she undid the chains on his ankles and then stretched his ankles to the bottom corners of the bed and snapped them in place as well. In seconds, he was chained spread-eagle on the bed with Mistress Cynthia on top of him, and he was blindfolded.

A laugh came from Mistress Cynthia. "Don't get your hopes up, slave. You'd have to do a hell of a lot more for me to deserve that."

She then climbed off him. "Your training is about to go into a new direction starting today," she said. She then ran her fingers up and down his right leg, stopping inches away from his groin and then moving back down to his feet again. "You need to understand the possibilities and the difficulties of being in such a relationship."

David realized there was no disguising his excitement to Mistress Cynthia. It was very obvious this whole thing excited him beyond belief, and it had been a very, very long time.

"I know what you are thinking," she said. "And contrary to what you believe, anything is possible here. But also, everything is earned. Everything!"

He felt the heat of this woman as she came into the proximity of his penis, and he almost couldn't contain himself, although the chains sort of made that an issue that he didn't really have to worry about. He had no idea what she was going to do, and then he felt a sharp intense pain on the skin around his balls as some kind of pinching type item, like a clothespin or something he couldn't recognize was placed there. Then another. And another. In a few moments, at least thirty of these items were placed all around his genital area, although fortunately not a single one on his penis itself.

Then one was added right on the tip.

It was not a clothespin. It was something specifically designed for this purpose alone as it bit and seemed to do it in a way to indicate that it was contoured in a way that it would continue to cause pain but not random pain as a simple clothespin would have done.

Then, when this was finished, he heard the last words of Mistress Cynthia on the subject of what she was doing. "Good night, slave. Sleep well."

She then placed a pillow under his neck. "I wouldn't want you getting uncomfortable while you slept." And then, as far as David could tell, she left him tied up for the night.

Chapter XIV

A lot of submissives and slaves fantasize about sleeping spread-eagle, tied up by a beautiful woman, but very few of them have probably ever experienced the sensation first-hand, or they experienced moments of it where it ended far sooner than what ended up being the entire night. And the addition of pain probably would not make things better either. But people rarely think of these things when planning for a night of bondage; they think of the excitement and then sort of neglect thinking about how hard something like that might really be. That was sort of what David was going through that evening.

At first, the whole experience was quite exciting, because he kept imagining Mistress Cynthia coming back and doing all sorts of evil things to him, even though experience here told him that probably wouldn't be the greatest thing to happen. But for a hardened submissive, it is very hard not to think about such things in fantasy terms. Well, at least until the things actually start to happen.

David was reminded of a session he had with Mistress Dominique early in his days of being her houseboy. During that time, there was a lot of cleaning, and a lot of serving, and the playing was pretty rare at that. This was a woman who worked very hard dominating men and women all day long, so much that it was often pretty rare for her to come back to her normal life and then want to keep doing the same thing to her houseboy who was "only here to serve you, Mistress". However, there were times when she did make the time for him, and those times were usually quite significant in both impact and excitement for the two of them.

During the earlier days of his houseboy status, she had a tendency of locking him in the dark, downstairs cage and leaving him for a few hours while she entertained clients. She would sometimes come out of her sessions (often to grab other equipment during scenes) and then check on him and sometimes tease him mercilessly just because she could. However, on this one day, she had been playing with him before one of her sessions, and she had been using a stock and bonds item that locked one's hands in a stock device much like a medieval stock but without the stand that went with it, meaning the device could be used in a portable manner as well. It was one of those devices hard-core subs really liked, and they would request it personally. On this day, however, Mistress Dominique was in a real bondage mood, and she placed David in it, loving the fact that it was like wearing a big piece of wood that acted like an uncomfortable pair of handcuffs. As one might expect, she liked placing it behind his back and his hands through the wrist slots so that she could have unfettered access to his private parts with him unable to resist anything she wanted to do. Not that he would have ever resisted her anyway, but part of the fantasy sometimes was giving the impression that the submissive might resist, and therefore, she was cutting out all chances of that action as well. Total control can be mental many times, but Mistress Dominique learned a long time ago that sometimes it helps to make it physical as well, just to remind a slave that it is real and not just some game, even if it is just some game in certain circumstances. Power games are kind of strange that way.

On this particular day, David, who was being released from the stocks by Mistress Dominique before her one o'clock appointment (often lovingly referred to as "my one o'clock"), came up with an interesting idea for reasons even he didn't know why. Mistress Dominique demanded total honesty from him at all times, and it was probably just one of those moments where he felt she would want to hear all that he had to say. He suggested that the stocks be kept on the other side of the cell door bars, so that his hands would be locked and fettered to the cell door bars themselves; this way he would be secured in bondage, locked to the cell's door and immobile at the same time as well. She thought about it for a moment and then said: "Get in the cage."

He moved into the cage, and then she closed the door, locking it and walking the key to the other side of the room so that he would have no possibility of reaching it. A long time ago, a submissive she was training to be her eventual personal slave, actually managed to reach the key and let himself out of the cage to go to the bathroom once. While she understood the need the slave had to use the restroom, there was just no excusing that action. She dismissed the slave forever and made sure that the key was never accessible to another slave again.

"Lay on your back and then put your hands through the bars," she said. He did it and then she locked him into the wrist slots of the stocks. "My session is three hours. You're going to be in this position for a long time, slave," she said.

"Yes, Mistress," said David, meekly. He craved bondage at this period in his life, and this just seemed like a wonderful circumstance. The added beauty of this particular cage was that it was located next to the room where Mistress Dominique held many of her sessions with her clients, and he quite often could hear full dialogue of these sessions that she held, and they were always quite exciting. Sometimes, she would come to him and talk about what excited her in some of these sessions and she would watch him to see what did and did not excite him. For the most part, she was a wonderful tease, and she loved to excite David to no end.

After Mistress Dominique closed the thick blue curtain in front of the cage and turned off the light to the dungeon that housed the cage before opening and closing the door that led to the hall, David was left in complete darkness. This was not your usual sense of darkness with a little light peeking in from outside. It was dead darkness where the only sign of light was the one in your mind, remembering light that once existed.

For David, this was exciting. He was naked, collared and tied up. Granted, he wasn't being sexually satisfied from the experience, but unlike a lot of misconceptions that believe bdsm slavery is filled with tons of sex, this was something he had come to grow quite used to. Mistress Dominique often ordered him to not whack off for days at a time until he was on his knees in front of her, and sometimes she didn't give him the opportunity then either. In the very beginning, he used to whack off anyway, but after a few months of being her house slave, or houseboy, he started to realize that he was probably going to get very little out of such a relationship if he didn't take it seriously. So he did.

On this day, however, the opportunity to whack off wasn't even a possibility as there was no way he could reach down with his hands locked to the outside of the cage in the stocks. It was exciting and frustrating at the exact same time. It is kind of hard to explain until someone has experienced the same sensation as well.

For about fifteen minutes, his mind wandered in the dark, and he began to fantasize all sorts of things. He imagined the directions this relationship might take, and he also began to remember some of the very intimate moments that he had shared with Mistress Dominique during the short time he had been her houseboy and the numerous sessions he had paid for before achieving that status with her. He remembered the first time she met him at the door (he had never seen her in person but had been relying on a two-dimensional photograph in an alternative lifestyles newspaper that indicated she was extremely beautiful, and the ad copy indicated she was both sensuous and cruel, something that opened up a piece of his mind that had never been used before, and he knew, ten seconds after looking at that picture, that this woman was the one he had to meet. But when he met her at the front door, she was dressed in a very revealing corset and hose, and she was far more beautiful than even the picture had revealed. She listened to his fantasies and then went to change clothes so she could be the fantasy he was seeking. At least that's how it all started. After some time, she and he realized there was far more to their inter-actions than laundry lists of what he wanted done to him, and they began to truly explore. The houseboy situation came not much long after that time of only a few years.

He thought back on the times that he had spent as her house-boy before the stocks were placed on his wrists. As a houseboy, he was always under the impression that he was to be her slave, but it didn't turn out that way. There were five other women working at the bondage establishment she owned, and the houseboy was essen-tially a free-for-all when Mistress Dominique was away or working with another client. Most of the girls, submissive, switches and dominants, tended to want foot massages or regular massages for the most part. Some wanted someone on which to practice whipping technique, and other times some just wanted some guy around they could talk to, or ask questions of, knowing he was not going to turn into some alpha male that needed to pee on his territory. And then there was Talia, Mistress Talia.

Mistress Talia was a woman from Mainland China who came to America during her childhood. She started out as Mistress Dominique's personal slave in the beginning, but Mistress Dominique saw some-thing else in her, a certain sense of control that very few other girls had who were in the care of Mistress Dominique. So Mistress Dominique stopped having Talia do submissive sessions and trained her to be a dominant. As expected, she was highly sought after by many, many clients who visited Mistress Dominique's establishment, and it was known all around town that Mistress Talia was both playful and extremely cruel.

Fast-forward a few years to the position of David as Mistress

Dominique's houseboy, and the situation for David suddenly became very important when it concerned the introduction of Mistress Talia. It was known by both Mistress Dominique and Mistress Talia that when David first started having sessions with Mistress Dominique, she was a very hard woman to schedule a session with, so at one point, David gave up and then decided to schedule a session with Mistress Talia, someone he found both enticing and quite frightening. This was on a day that Mistress Dominique had decided to take the day off, and when David's call came for booking a session with Mistress Dominique, he was informed she was not available so he made the session with Mistress Talia instead; he had never scheduled with anyone but Mistress Dominique during the two years he had been coming to Mistress Dominique's house of bondage. When David arrived on the premises, he was met at the door by Mistress Talia who then ushered him into the receiving room and then left him there, as if she would return momentarily and they would discuss what would be their first session together. However, instead of Mistress Talia returning, Mistress Dominique returned, stating that she realized he was coming in, and she decided to not take the time off and actually do the session with him. It was the first time that David realized there was something slightly significant happening between him and Mistress Dominique; and as David would come to realize years later, Mistress Dominique had realized on that one day that avoiding that one session would have lost her future slave forever. After that day, up until the day David became a houseboy, he always received a smile from Mistress Talia but very little else.

When David became the houseboy, all of that changed. Mistress Talia was the first one to use the houseboy. Before that, it was pretty much a given that the houseboy was Mistress Dominique's responsibility because there was something personal going on between them, although previous houseboys had pretty much been open game but pretty much ignored because most tended to be more problematic than desirable anyway. But David was different. Mistress Talia started during one of Mistress Dominique's three hour sessions with a client. She told David to massage her feet, and then she began berating him over how to properly massage a mistress's feet, even grabbing his feet at one time and massaging them so he knew what she was talking about. She was mean and harsh and outright violent to him most of the time. One evening, he was locked in the cage where a session was going to be going on in the next room and Mistress Talia left her client for a moment to enter the darkened room, closing the door behind her so it was completely dark when she entered the room with the cage that held David. She got up close to the cage door, so close that David could smell her perfume and knew immediately whom it was. She spoke in that seductive voice she used all the time around clients, and she spared him nothing as she used it on him. She said: "Slave, I am going to be holding a session in the next room, and that means you need to be quiet. If I so much as hear you breathe once, I'm going to come back in here, string you up from the ceiling and see how many pieces of your skin I can pull off your body before Mistress Dominique figures out what I've done to you. But I promise you, she won't be fast enough to save your sorry ass. Am I making myself perfectly clear, slave?"

"Yes, Mistress," said David, not even realizing at that time that Mistress Talia was the only woman in the employ of Mistress Dominique to whom he addressed only as Mistress rather than by name.

She remained there for a moment and said nothing. Then she spoke one more time. "One peep. One sound. Your stomach settling. Anything. And I'm coming back for you." There was a long pause and still no sound of her leaving the room. She added: "Then again, I might just come back and do it anyway." Then she left and went to go do her session.

For the next hour or so, David found himself avoiding making any sounds, even though he suspected that Mistress Talia would not have heard a thing. He really felt that it was not worth taking a chance. Unlike the other women that worked at Mistress Dominique's establishment, Mistress Talia didn't make idle threats; when she threatened a slave with something sinister, that slave either took her seriously or that slave suffered in ways he or she never before imagined. Mistress Talia was out of school sick the day the concept of mercy was taught to dominant women.

One evening, after only a few weeks of David being the houseboy, Mistress Talia decided to have fun with the houseboy, and started to make his life miserable. It was a house rule at Mistress Dominique's place that if David wanted to use the restroom, he needed to get permission from Mistress Dominique, and if Mistress Dominique was occupied at that moment, he was allowed to ask permission from any of the women working in the place, kind of in a hierarchy of decision-making (asking the dominant women first and then going down the list to the submissive women if none of the dominant ones were available; the rule was always accepted that even though the submissive women working at the place were submissive, David was never to assume a posture that indicated that they were ever lower caste than he was; David was as low in status as you could be in the eyes of everyone who worked for Mistress Dominique, and that was how it was meant to be). Well, one day, David wandered into the reclining room where the women took calls for potential sessions. He needed to use the restroom. He was naked like always, a collar around his neck, although he was not in any type of bondage but wore the mandatory wrist and ankle cuffs in case a woman might want to lock him to something or in some position at any one time. Mistress Constance and Mistress Talia were both sitting on the plush sofa that took up about half the room, and Loralee, a switch was sitting on the carpet going through an old photo album of which David didn't have the opportunity to see what the photos happened to be (sometimes a houseboy wasn't allowed to be a part of all the fun at the house). David addressed Mistress Constance, even though she was seated further away from him than was Mistress Talia; David went out of his way to avoid Mistress Talia whenever possible, and that was certainly not a secret to the amused women that worked at the house.

"Mistress Constance, may I have permission to speak?" This was the only phrase he was allowed to use around the women of the house, unless there was a fire or something of that nature, and it was often thought by David that even an emergency wouldn't be enough for some of these women.

Mistress Constance stared at him for a second and then turned to Mistress Talia and smiled. "Should I give him permission?"

Mistress Talia grinned that evil grin she seemed to always wear when David was around. "Yes, I wouldn't miss what he has to say for anything."

Mistress Constance turned back to David. "Yes, slave, you may speak."

"Mistress Constance, may I please use the restroom?"

She just stared at him. "You interrupted a conversation between two mistresses to ask to go to the bathroom?"

It was another one of those situations to which David did not have a good enough answer, something he grew quite used to in this house. "Yes, Mistress Constance," he said.

She continued to stare at him. "How bad do you have to go?"

His eyes opened wide. Not once did they ever say no. Well, aside from Mistress Talia that is. It was almost always just a formality. "Very bad, Mistress Constance."

She shook her head. "Let me know when you're about to explode. Very bad is not a good enough reason." She then turned back to Mistress Talia and continued a conversation they had been having.

David stood there for a few moments, unsure of what to say. He needed to use the restroom. Then, to his horror, his surprised gaze was met by a matter-of-factly gaze worn on the face of Mistress Talia. "Did you not hear Mistress Constance, slave? Did you want to join our conversation and be one of the girls? Have you forgotten who and what you are here?"

"No, Mistress," he said. "I apologize."

"Then get the fuck out of here," said Mistress Talia.

"You may return when you are ready to explode," said Mistress Constance. The two mistresses started to laugh with each other and then continued on with their conversation from before.

David stood silently for a second, stunned at the strange attitude. They'd never actually been like this before. Then a voice he rarely heard spoke up, the voice of Loralee, the switch. "David, if you value your life, I'd head upstairs and start dusting the interrogation room like Mistress Talia originally told you to do."

"Yes, Mistress Loralee," said David as he rushed out of the room, not missing the laughing that came from the women, including Loralee.

That wasn't the end of it, of course. After he went back upstairs to continue working on the interrogation room, a very dark, sinister looking dungeon with all sorts of bondage equipment, racks, pulleys and everything of that nature, he started to feel that he really, really had to go to the bathroom. After about ten minutes, he realized that he could take no more and rushed back downstairs to ask permission yet again. To his joyous surprise, he arrived to see only Mistress Constance and Loralee in the reclining room. Mistress Talia was nowhere in sight. He asked again.

"Are you about to explode?" said Mistress Constance.

"Yes, Mistress Constance," as he tried to stand straight as required, even though it was getting hard to do so."

Mistress Constance turned to Loralee. "What do you think?"

"Yes, Mistress," said Loralee, "I think he should be allowed."

Mistress Constance turned back to David. "You have my permission. Use the downstairs bathroom."

"Thank you, Mistress Constance," said David as he turned to leave.

"Hold on," said Mistress Constance. She held out her hand. David moved forward and kissed it until she retrieved it and turned away from him. Then he rushed to go use the restroom. That was the thing about Mistress Constance; she always had some kind of formality to everything she did. Some people said that was what seemed to attract some very high-class clients to her over the few years she had been doing the domination thing.

David got to the stairway heading downstairs to the restroom when he heard Mistress Talia's voice over even the sounds of men being beat in nearby dungeons, so loud he assumed even people in sessions heard it.

"YOU WHAT?" she yelled. "WHERE IS HE?"

David didn't hear the response, but he assumed that they were talking about him, so being in dire need of having to urinate, he ran down the stairs and headed for the restroom. He only got halfway down the carpeted stairs when he heard the sound of Mistress Talia's boots pounding on the hardwood floors of the kitchen, right around the corner of the stairway. David dived into the restroom and threw up the seat so he could urinate, hoping Mistress Talia was nowhere in sight.

Well, that did not work out as hoped. He barely started to urinate when he could feel the presence of Mistress Talia standing directly behind him. She said one word.

"Stop."

He did as he was told. She walked around him and then stared down at his penis, laughing as she did so. "Okay, go ahead," she said, her eyes glaring down at his manhood.

As bad as David wanted to go, he couldn't. Having Mistress Talia stare at him when he tried froze him up completely.

She coyly ran her index finger across her lips. "Are we having trouble pissing in front of a woman now, slave?"

David just bowed his head. He knew he was not going to be

able to do it. And he knew she knew that as well.

"I guess you don't really have to go then, slave," she said. "Either do it now, or get back to work."

He tried as hard as he could, but it just wouldn't happen. To make matters worse, he was getting hard as well, and any chance of pissing was dying really fast. "Mistress, this isn't fair."

Now, there were any number of things she could have done to him for speaking out of turn, or saying what he did, but she just laughed instead. "Perhaps you should understand that sometimes it's not meant to be fair. There are some very sensuous mistresses, like Mistress Dominique, who you will devote your entire life to, and she will care about how you like it. And then there are mistresses like me. I want to see you suffer. It gives me pleasure like you could never imagine. As long as I have a voice in how we treat you here, you will always know that I will take every bit of pleasure in making your life a living hell. Sometimes, a guy like you needs a woman like me. Remember that in the future when you make the mistake of serving the wrong woman."

He wasn't sure what she meant. But there was little time to reflect on it.

"Scoot, back upstairs, you. When you finally think you are able to urinate, I order you to come directly to me, not to any of the other mistresses or subs here. Me. Unless you can wait another two hours for Mistress Dominique to get out of her session, and I may just let her know what I've commanded so she'll probably back me on it anyway."

David just stared at her. "Mistress Talia, why are you doing this to me?"

She just stared back at him. "Because I care about you, David. Now back up to the interrogation room." She patted his behind and sent him on his way.

All of these things went through David's head as he was left alone in that dark cage for the first fifteen minutes or so, and then that was when he started to realize he made a mistake. His wrists were locked in the stocks on the other side of the cell's door, and he never realized the significance of the stocks in being kept in this position. Had there been no stocks, and his wrists were locked together on the other side of the cell's door, his arms would have been flat on the carpet outside the cage, and it would be frustrating, but it would not be that uncomfortable. However, with the stocks, his wrists were elevated slightly off the carpet, by about five of six inches, so his shoulders were now forced into a position where his arms started to ache. And then his back started to ache as well because of the strange angle that his arms were pushed into.

This was only about fifteen minutes into the bondage situation that he realized he was starting to feel uncomfortable. And Mistress Dominique was going to be in a session for three hours, but there was no guarantee that she would come out and check on him like she did sometimes but not during some of the more intense sessions that she put clients through.

Thirty minutes into the situation, it became an ordeal. His arms were really in throbbing pain. He began trying to lift his legs so that his legs were parallel to his arms, practically forcing his legs through the cell door itself. It offered him a few moments of the pain going away, but then it became very uncomfortable trying to get his legs to the area where his head was, something more designed for a gymnast than a corporate stockbroker.

For the next two hours, he would trade between swollen pain in his arms and his back in serious pain as an attempt to cut down on the swelling. And during this time, not once did Mistress Dominique show up to take a break during her long session.

He had no concept of time, but he only knew it had been a very long time, and he was almost becoming a blithering idiot as he realized how hopeless his situation was for him. It was pain unlike any that had ever been inflicted on him; it was continuous and not the pleasurable kind of pain that seems to be incorporated in sadomasochism, pain inflicted as part of a session, even though this was pain inflicted as part of a session.

As he thought about it, he realized why it was not pleasurable pain, aside from the throbbing. His mistress had no idea she was putting him through pain. Yes, she had put him through hell many times before, but this was the first time that she was inflicting unbearable pain upon him and not even being aware of her sadism. It was pain with no purpose but to hurt, causing no one any pleasure in the process.

This went on forever, at least in David's world, and at one point, while he was pretty much talking to himself in tongues, she finally arrived, opening the door and heard him whimpering in the cage. She came over immediately, flicked on a lamp and then looked at him.

"What's wrong, David?"

He explained quickly what had happened. She began to unlock the stocks and then unlocked the cell's door so she could get at him. His upper body was practically numb at the time, and he could barely move his hands or arms. She wrapped him up in her arms and held him tight for what had to be the longest time she'd ever held him intimately. Slowly, the pain began to subside, and he could move his hands again. Then she said the moral of the story to him as she rocked him back and forth in her arms in front of the door of the cell that housed that pain: "Let this be a lesson to you, slave. Always be careful what you ask for because you might just get it, and it might not be what you're expecting." It was such a stupid sounding moral that both of them started laughing, and they didn't stop for a long time.

He never suggested a bondage situation again.

All of these memories went through David's mind as he was spread-out, tied up on the bed Mistress Cynthia put him on. He couldn't sleep; he was too excited to sleep. When tied up like this, it can sometimes be very difficult to turn off one's mind, and the mind has a habit of influencing the lower part of the body, and once one's sporting a hard-on that just won't go away, sleep just doesn't seem to want to come.

So David remained without sleep for most of the night, knowing there was little he could do to influence his mind from thinking nothing but thoughts that only served to get him more excited. Finally, at one point, he must have dozed off, but with the blindfold and the restraints, it was really hard to tell what was sleep, what was part of his subconscious and what was him, helpless in bed thrashing back and forth totally awake and fearful of what was going to happen next.

Chapter XV

Morning. The first sign of daylight. The two usually go together. Unfortunately, for David, morning came but there was no sign of light. The blindfold cut out any chance of observing that. It was a lot like the many nights that Mistress Dominique used to keep him tied up in the basement cell in the blue draped dungeon. He never knew when it was morning, and there was never a clock to tell or a single drop of light to indicate that night was over and day had begun. He relied on Mistress Dominique almost every morning to know that his evening had ended and a new day had begun. It was quite disorienting, but it was the way Mistress Dominique felt he needed to learn how to be in one's complete control.

This morning, however, was not like the ones he remembered when waking up in the personal care of Mistress Dominique. No, as a matter of fact, it was only a few seconds after he woke up that he realized how different it was.

Mistress Dominique had a pleasant habit of turning on an outside lamp and then slowly acclimating him to his environment before sitting outside his cage in the still darkened room and asking him to relate his dreams to her and his current thoughts on whatever was going through his mind. Sometimes, she would share her own thoughts or maybe her own dreams if they seemed to relate to something that would be of interest to him and use to her in relating it to him.

When David woke up this morning while tied spread-eagle to the bed, it was not a soft, sensuous voice that brought him to consciousness. No, it was the pain caused from a whip that striped across his inner thigh. And then that same whip against his other thigh, and then a series of others that felt completely indiscriminate in where they landed, at least until the last one landed across his crotch, throwing his defenses into spasms of pain and his mind into a mode of desperate violation.

"I thought that would wake you, slave," said the voice of the only woman he had come to know in the last few months. How he dreaded that voice. Now, with his privates completely exposed, more than ever.

"I have a treat for you, slave," she said as she brought the whip down one more time on his chest, causing a sharp pain and then a gasp of coolness in the same spot, indicating that she probably got blood on that last hit. Being completely subdued as he was and unable to see a single thing, he knew better than to mumble through the hood, so he waited to hear what she had to say.

Instead of the whip coming across his body again, he felt her soft hand slowly rub across his chest, making wide circles as she started moving down towards his stomach and then continued down further and further until she was within reach of making David a very happy slave. "I am completely naked," she said. "I thought that if I was going to play with you like this, you might like to know that your mistress is exposed and just as vulnerable as you are."

The big difference was: he couldn't see her.

She rubbed all around his penis, touching every spot around it but not touching it at all. She ran her fingers over some of the clips that were holding him, and each time she came close to one of them, David wanted to scream out in terror because it was like she was pulling his insides out through his skin each time she did. Yet, the clips remained where they were, and she continued to play with his exposed, vulnerable body.

"I bet you wish you could see me right now, don't you?" she said.

"Yes, Mistress Cynthia." He wasn't lying. He really wished he could see her. She might have been some kind of demon from hell, but she was extremely beautiful, and she was the only woman with whom he'd had any significant contact over the last two months. Well, aside from his one massage of Mistress Dominique, but for some reason that seemed to feel more like a dream than a recent reality, so it was even hard to equate that with anything but a quick moment of pleasure in a sea of disparity.

"Okay, I'll make you a deal. I'm going to pull each of these clips from your body, and if you don't make a single sound, I'll let you see me naked."

David said nothing. While he wanted to see her in all her glory, he certainly did not relish what it was going to feel like to have those clips removed from his body, especially since they had been causing him pain all night long. Then again, common sense told him that eventually they had to come off, so perhaps getting something out of it might make it all worth it. Okay, it might not make it all worth it, but when one has been tied up and tortured all night long, one starts to look for the pleasant things no matter how hard one has to imagine them.

"Do we have a deal, slave?" she said.

"Yes, Mistress Cynthia," he replied.

Then there was silence. Deadening silence. Then a few moments later, he heard the sound of her feet as they walked across the wooden floor, moving around the bed. Yes, he could hear feet on the floor. Not shoes, boots or high heels. He was beginning to believe that perhaps she was naked.

Then he felt her weight as she climbed onto the bed and straddled his chest like she had done the night before. Then there was an intense pinching pressure on the skin below his penis, where one of the many clips was located. She squeezed in on the clip, forcing it to bite tighter than before. He gasped as she did it.

"David, this is only the first one, and I haven't even removed it yet. Don't you want to see me naked?"

"Yes, Mistress Cynthia."

"Then shut the fuck up and don't make a sound. Do I make myself completely clear?"

"Yes, Mistress Cynthia," he replied quickly.

There was a long silence before she spoke again. "Perhaps I am making this too easy for you. As it is, you have nothing to lose. If you make no sound, you get the privilege of seeing me naked. If you make a sound, you still get the clips removed from your body. Perhaps we should have some type of real incentive for you to remain silent." There was an even longer pause this time. Even though he was unable to see a single thing, he actually believed he could hear a smile come to her face before she spoke again. "This house is quite unique in all that it has to offer. On the lower level, there are a series of cells that are quite uncomfortable. I'm sure you've fantasized about these kinds of cells, but you've never been in any like them for any length of time, so let's just say that reality and fantasy can sometimes not be the same thing. Anyway, here's my offer to you should you decide to accept it, and as death is the only way you can't accept it, here goes: If you do not succeed in making no sound up until the last clip is pulled from your body, I am going to lock you into the most solitary of those cells, tied up much like you are tied right now, put through pain like you've never experienced before, fed less than the gruel you're getting now, and sentenced to two weeks of this without ever seeing the light of day until I'm satisfied that you have paid for your crime." There was another long pause. "And we're going to have to introduce the concept of chastity to you, slave. Even though I know you haven't orgasmed since you've been here, I think we need to keep that little erection of yours a bit more under control. Unfortunately, that's going to be something you're going to experience regardless of how well you do."

She shifted her weight on his body. From what David could fathom, she was situated over him so that she was in perfect position to start pulling clips from his body. "I'm only going to say this once," she said. "One sound, and you lose."

Then she pulled a clip from right below his cock and tossed it aside. His whole body went through spasms as he heard the sound of the clip hitting the wooden floor. He almost gasped from the sharp pain, but he bit his tongue and then he realized he was almost about to cry out as the throbbing started echoing through his groin area from the skin as it started to expand back out again in very tiny increments, taking forever to do so with each second hurting more than the last.

She laughed. "That was fun. Too bad the hood on your head makes it so I can't see you cry. But then, that might not work in your favor." She didn't even give him a chance to register her words before she pulled off a second one from almost the same spot. And then one above his cock. And then one to the right side of it.

The pain was unbelievable. Sharp, biting pain that ripped through his skin and throbbed as more and more of the clips were pulled from his skin, causing a sensation of horror that didn't seem to subside because each time it felt like it might, she would pull a few more clips again. He had no idea how many clips she had originally put on him, but pulling them off seemed to take forever, and the more he squirmed and struggled against his bonds, the more she pulled, and the more she laughed.

At one point, David actually thought he was going to pass out, and almost as if reading his mind, she stopped. She then began rubbing her soft hands across his swollen groin area, bumping into his hardened member that must have been standing like a lighthouse around a very tiny island cause she seemed to be bumping into it more and more as she massaged his sore skin. It was driving him out of his mind the more she kept touching him there.

"Don't fall asleep on me, slave," she said. "There's a lot more to go, and I'm nowhere near tired yet."

She continued pulling them off him. For some reason, it was even worse during the second wave of clips. She had a nasty habit of grabbing them and squeezing in on them and then jerking them off him instead of releasing the clips instead. It was quite obvious that she knew exactly how to make the experience worse on someone, and if there was an easier way of doing it, she was doing everything possible to make sure she didn't accidentally do it that way.

She stopped again when he felt his consciousness floating back and forth. It was hard to tell what was going on half the time, aside from the pain, because of his inability to move at all and the fact that the hood seemed to deprive him of most senses.

"I know this is hurting you, slave, and I'd like to say something reassuring like it hurts me more than it does you to do this to you, but I'd be lying. I bet it hurts a lot, and to be honest, I love doing this to you." Then she continued pulling more of the clips from his body. Through it all, he did everything possible to make sure he didn't make a sound.

"Wow, you're down to five more," she said after another rest. "These five are really going to suck. I'd hate to be you. But then again, I don't have the appendage you do that's so fun to do this to."

The first one was one right below his cock. He had no idea where there were clips anymore because so many had been removed, and he was feeling nothing but throbbing pain throughout that entire section of his body. She squeezed in on it really hard and then jerked it off his body so hard that he felt that she was pulling half the skin with it as well.

He practically bit his lip off during the process, but he made no sound.

"Very good, slave," she said. "Unfortunately, that was the easy one." She then wrapped her hands around three of them and jerked them off all at the same time. This time, he remembered little after.

All he remembered was Mistress Cynthia slapping his stomach over and over again, not really for causing pain, but just to get his attention. He then realized he must have passed out.

"That was a really good way of avoiding speaking," she said. "Got to admire it. Unfortunately, there's one more, and it's on the tip of your cock. That must hurt like a mother."

It did. With all the others gone, he still felt their pain, but he was quite aware of that one still on him. It was so tight on his skin that it appeared to be a badly conducted piercing rather than a clip. He was not looking forward to it being removed.

"This one's going to suck, David. I don't know an easier way to say it than that."

He took a deep breath and held it. There was no pressure on it, just a laugh from Mistress Cynthia. She was obviously taking great pleasure in his present and future discomfort.

Then she ripped it off him, drawing what had to be a ton of hair and some blood at the same time. He was about to scream, ripping the bonds from the bed and run from this place, but all he managed to do was jerk in his bonds and he bit down so hard on his lip that he was definitely drawing blood. But he made no sound.

"Wow, I'm really impressed, slave. You didn't make a single sound."

David relaxed his body for a second and took in all the pain, meanwhile knowing that he had succeeded. It was a rare victory, but it was such a great one for him. For the first time since coming to this place he felt—

--Pain. Pain like he had never felt before. Where his skin had been throbbing from the clips before, he felt a sudden flash of intense pain as what seemed to be three more clips were ripped from his body on the skin of his scrotum, drawing blood in the process.

He squirmed and screamed at the same time. He hadn't been expecting the flash of pain. This came from nowhere.

All he heard was the laughter from Mistress Cynthia. "I was a really bad girl. I forgot I left those three on you for last. Bet you weren't expecting that."

He felt betrayed. She had told him that the one on his cock had been the last one. This just wasn't fair. He wasn't expecting those last three, and he'd been so overcome with the pain from the rest that he didn't even know they were still on him.

She clucked her tongue. "What a shame. You were so close. You almost earned the privilege of seeing me naked. Instead, you're going to be put through hell for the next two weeks. Just because you couldn't control your big mouth. I really feel for you, David, but you disappointed me, and now you must suffer for doing so. When will you ever learn?"

Then she climbed off him, and from what he could hear, she left the room, closing the door behind her.

He wasn't sure whether to be disappointed in himself for failing or for actually believing that for once Mistress Cynthia was going to reward him for doing the best he could.

Chapter XVI

To David's surprise, his failure did not immediately bring upon the wrath of Mistress Cynthia. No, actually, she did the complete opposite of what he was expecting: she told him to rest and left him alone in his world of darkness, still tied to the bed. Even after she said this was what she was going to do, leave him alone for awhile, he maintained a state of alertness, convinced she was going to pounce on him when he was least expecting it. But after an unbelievable amount of time, he began to believe that perhaps she was serious, and even though he was sexually stimulated and excited at the same time, he eventually began to calm down and rest, knowing that he would probably need every ounce of rest he could get.

He did not know how long he had been lying there since he last heard Mistress Cynthia speak, but after some time his mind stopped playing tricks on him, imagining she was right there in the room with him, and he actually managed to doze off. It was probably due more to exhaustion than anything else, but at one point he lost consciousness and finally reached the one state of being where he could not be touched by Mistress Cynthia or any of the women in the employee of Mistress Dominique.

Well, at least that's how it would appear. Of course, David always knew that he was never going to really be free, no matter how supposed that freedom might appear to him, like in the few hours of sleep he achieved during a lull in what was happening to him. That was probably never more realized by him than when he managed to finally wake up from the tiny bit of sleep he did receive at this particular time.

"Wakey, wakey, David," said Mistress Cynthia in that soft tone of speaking she liked to use when she was indicating that all was not as pleasant as her voice was making circumstances seem. "Let's not forget you lost your one chance at the brass ring today. Unfortunately, you have to pay the price for your failure."

David struggled momentarily and it didn't take much thrashing back and forth for him to realize that he was still locked down as he had been before. However, something seemed different, although he couldn't immediately put his finger on what that thing was.

The mid-section of his body was still in great pain from the clip session just a few hours before (he was assuming it was a few hours; it was practically impossible to tell time in this place without even light peeking through the hood to give him a clue), but something down there seemed different than before. Then, as usually happened to him when he started to get excited about his circumstances, he began to feel the blood fill into his organ and it start to stiffen like usual. And then, instead of that frustrating sensation of being excited and not being able to do anything about it, he felt a jolt of pain from the top side of his penis, which was immediately followed by the lower side of it as well. For some reason, he couldn't get hard, and his cock was doing everything physically possible to do so. For some reason, there was no room for him to stretch it out; instead, it was stuck, and he was growing even more excited without the ability to present that excitement through the natural stretching process.

"Never wore a chastity device before, David?" she said.

And then he understood everything. No, he had never worn one before. There was one attempt a long time ago when Mistress Dominique tried to slip one onto him after he'd given her one of his famous massages, and she wanted to repay him by forcing him into a state of continuous arousal denial (rewards in the kinky world can be strange that way), but no matter what she did, she could not get him soft enough to slip him into the contraption. Every time she gave him some time to calm down, she would try to put it on him again and he would get excited too fast for her to be able to finish the job. It was probably as frustrating for her as it was for him. At one point, she stated that she was going to wait until he was asleep and put him in it then, but that moment never came, so David sort of assumed she had forgotten all about it.

"Yes, David," said Mistress Cynthia, "I know all about the failures you and your mistress have had in this area in the past. Did you honestly think she would have me train you for her and not divulge everything about you, including your previous training?"

For some reason, David was under the impression that this training he was receiving from Mistress Cynthia was in no way connected to any communication with Mistress Dominique. It did not make any sense for it to be that way, as it was obvious that Mistress Cynthia was training him for Mistress Dominique and not just for the sake of training alone. Still, it never seemed to really resonate in David that this was all tied together, that what one woman did to him here was in every way related to what another might be planning for him as well. One night, before putting David asleep, Mistress Cynthia had summed it up, and surprisingly, it was one of those comments that David found hot, but never realized the significance of it. She said: "Never think of me as someone different than your mistress. She and I are one and the same. Understand that, and you will understand that to truly learn to be the slave you were meant to be is to give up the belief that it should have ever been any other way."

It sounded like double-speak at the time, but it was starting to make a lot more sense now.

"Now listen, David, because I am only going to say this once," said his captress. "The chastity device is for your own good. You are going to be alone for a long time, and what often happens is a slave begins to excite himself due to the lack of outside stimulation and the fantasies that are going through his head. Sometimes, not always, but sometimes, even the sturdiest of slaves cannot resist pleasuring himself, and then when I finally come to check up on him, let's just say that his potential is completely lost, and I can do nothing less than to either start him over at the beginning, BEFORE he even arrived here, or just to declare him unfit and let Mistress Dominique decide whether or not you are worth salvaging, selling off, or letting go completely. To be honest, there have been a few failures here over the years, and let's just say that while it's the rarest choice ever made, letting one go is the least horrible thing that could happen to you."

David remained silent and made no attempt to move, even though he wouldn't have moved much if he wanted to anyway. Sometimes, it was hard to tell what was being told to him from a fantasy aspect and what was to be considered completely reality. The more he experienced at this place, the more he began to believe there was little fantasy and way too much reality.

"Now, I want you to understand that I am about to remove the bonds holding you down right now. As I do so, you are to remain stretched out completely and not move one iota during the time that I am unlocking you. I will tell you when to move. You do not move without me first stating so. Is that understood?"

"Yes, Mistress Cynthia," he mumbled through the hood.

"Very good," she said. He then felt the tightness of the bonds on his left wrist loosen a bit, and he realized if he wanted to he could probably pull his left hand to his chest and he would no longer be confined as he was a moment ago. But he remained still and held his hand out as far as it was before she undid the restraint. He might be in a lot of discomfort and pain, but he was not stupid; okay, maybe stupid judging from the predicament he was in at the moment but foolish was probably the better choice of word.

Then his right wrist was released. Then his left and right legs. For a moment, he just remained on his back, stretched as if he was still in restraints but too full of common sense to move a single bit.

"Good," she said. "Now, I want you to lift your left leg into the air and then bring it back down again."

He tried, but for some reason, he just couldn't get the energy to do so. He had a strong feeling he was going to be punished unmercifully for failing what she just told him to do. He flinched, figuring she was probably going to pull his teeth out with a rusty pair of pliers or something.

Instead, she laughed. "I wanted you to move your leg to see if you could. Relax, David. I'm not going to hurt you for doing something you can't do. Try to move your arms."

He tried to raise his right arm, and he was able to get a bit off the bed before his arm collapsed on the bed again. The awkward position of lying like he was, in heavy restraints as she kept him for a time period that he was not aware, had completely weakened him.

He felt her climb onto the bed and then on top of him again. It didn't take a genius to figure out that she was as naked as she had been before as he felt her soft skin against his. Then he felt something happen to his right arm that he hadn't expected: pleasure. She was rubbing his right arm, lifting it up into the air, dropping it back down and continuing to rub it. Quickly, to his complete surprise, he was beginning to feel life in his arm again. Then she moved to his other arm and continued doing the same thing to it. Then his legs as well.

It was highly erotic, and it was exciting him to no end, although each time he started to get excited, he felt that constriction of the chastity device against him, and he wanted to do anything necessary to get that thing removed. But he also realized that while Mistress Cynthia was being more than gracious with her generous application of pleasure on his limbs, the removal of that device was probably not one of the things she was willing to do for him. And he figured the discussion of it would probably make it far worse than it was already, so he remained silent on that one.

Finally, she stopped and climbed off him. "Stand up, slave."

Slowly, he maneuvered himself to his feet until he was in a somewhat standing position, resting his legs against the side of the bed for leverage. He felt a lot better, but he still felt like he was going to fall.

Then he felt a tug on the back of his neck as she stuck her fingers into the ring of his collar and pulled him forward towards her. He stumbled a bit from his weakened legs, but after a few moments, he found himself standing away from the bed without need of any support.

"You will follow me like you did before, slave," she said. "There is still the matter of your punishment which you still owe me." Then she grabbed his hands and forced them behind his back, locking them together as she had done before on the trip to the bed of restraint.

She led him out of the room, which he ascertained from the sound of the door opening and their movement in the direction of where he had heard it. Then she stopped for a moment and he heard the door slam shut behind them. Then it was a series of steps and lower landings until they had gone even further down than he remembered they had gone when coming up to the floor where she had kept him for however long she had kept him up there. Then they went down a number of flights until the carpeted stairway gave way to a hard, stone-like ground where he led him down a very long corridor.

He figured she was going to bring him into another room, assuming this was the basement of the house, but instead, he heard the sound of a door creaking and then they started down yet another set of stone stairs to yet another level lower than they were before. At this time, David heard something he hadn't been expecting. It was sound of whimpering from some distance away. Only, what shocked him was that the whimpering was coming from what appeared to be a woman.

David stopped dead in his tracks. Something just didn't seem right here.

Mistress Cynthia tugged on his collar as if to remind him why he was here and then stopped for a moment, apparently realizing why it was that David had stopped. "Men are not the only slaves trained here," she said. "Mistress Dominique believes that all dominants must first learn how to be good slaves."

David wondered if Mistress Cynthia had been a slave herself.

She started laughing. "God, you are so predictable. Yes, that's how I started here as well, even though I had been a professional dominant for a few years before coming here."

David wanted to ask a ton of questions about this place, about how it came to be, but he realized that he might never get that opportunity, no matter how much the questions burned into his mind. He just wanted to blurt out his questions about how such a place like this could exist, how it could have ever been started, and how come no one knew anything about it. But, unfortunately, the opportunity for him to ask questions of that nature had long been passed.

She continued to laugh. "And to answer the inevitable question that you will eventually ask, if you are not thinking it now, the answer is no. No man will ever be trained to be a dominant here. You, unfortunately, get to start off a slave, and if you work very hard, you get to remain one."

She maneuvered him down the corridor further, and he could hear the sound of the whimpering woman get louder the closer they came to wherever it was she was being kept. Then in true Doppler fashion, the sound of her whimpering teetered off and then dissipated as Mistress Cynthia moved him further down the hallway. Finally, she stopped and he stopped with a quick jerk of the finger in his collar, knowing she wanted him to move no further. "This will be your new home for the near future," she said.

Then, instead of hearing the sound of a door being opened, or anything that might sound closer to what one might consider livable, he heard the sound of keys and the clanking of a lock one would hear on a cell door. Even though Mistress Cynthia had told him that was pretty much what he was to expect, he just couldn't imagine that he was now about to be locked in some kind of cage by Mistress Cynthia for the allotted amount of time she had been talking about earlier. Even Mistress Dominique had never locked him in her house cage for any longer than a period of a day and a half (the one time of endurance that she had decided he needed to learn what it was like to be trapped within her clutches). Weeks just didn't seem possible, and he had a feeling that Mistress Cynthia wasn't exactly going to be very accommodating in how she treated him while he was trapped in this type of environment.

"In, slave," she said as she pulled tight on the ring of his collar and ushered him into what appeared to be a very cool room with very cold floors. She turned him around quickly, and then she threw him to the floor. Then he heard the sound of the cell door as she slammed it shut, which was immediately followed by the sound of a large set of keys turning over in the lock, quite obviously locking him in for whatever period of time she was intending to leave him in this place.

As David began to feel his way through the cell that he was placed into, trying to get a feel for what his new surroundings would be like, he heard the sound of the whimpering woman again. And then he heard something that brought immediate fear to him and everything he had left of himself in this dark, forbidding place. It was the voice of another woman, obviously addressing the whimpering female slave.

"Your pleas aren't going to do any good, Mary Ann," said the voice. "As a matter of fact, they only bring me pleasure to know that you're suffering and in way over your head and can't do a thing about getting out of this predicament. No one cares what happens to you here, except me, and I'm your worst enemy. One day, you might be on this side of the cage where I am, but you first have to live through what I have to give you, and believe you me that very few have ever succeeded." David could hear the laughter come from the woman as it was very obvious she knew how much power she was wielding at this particular time. "You can cry all you want, and you can scream all you want, but I promise you, nothing is going to stop me from having the time of my life with you while you are in my care. Let's just say that every slave who comes through here learns to fear my wrath at some time or another as this is MY prison, and no one gets an easy ride." There was a long pause. "Now, let's see what part of your skin I haven't managed to draw blood from yet."

David remained in silence and listened to the exchange in the other section of what this woman called "MY prison". At first, when the woman started, he thought this was the poor girl's dominant, much as Mistress Cynthia was David's present dominant. He was beginning to wonder if he was about to be put through the hell that this woman seemed to enjoy inflicting.

And that wasn't really bothered him. David was convinced that for the most part, it didn't really matter which dominant was torturing him or putting him through hell because Mistress Cynthia pretty much proved to him that it didn't matter what he thought; his experience here was going to suck regardless. What really bothered him was the realization that he recognized that woman's voice. It was a voice he had feared so many times in his past.

He was housed in the prison (MY PRISON) of none other than Mistress Talia, and he realized that once she discovered who he was, life was going to become even worse than the horrors promised to him by Mistress Cynthia.

Chapter XVII

The fear that David had about Mistress Talia discovering him and then making his life miserable didn't exactly come to be realized. The reason for that was not that Mistress Talia was kept unaware of the fact that David was in her prison, but the fact that no one came to visit him aside from a few visits from Mistress Cynthia at very odd times.

For the first day and night, and probably a little time beyond that, David was kept in the darkness of this caged environment that was only further darkened by the hood that Mistress Cynthia kept over his head. He could see nothing, and all he could do was hear things going on. He had no sense of time as he would if he had access to a clock, but he began to time his existence by listening to the screams of the poor woman that appeared to be the only other prisoner of this part of the establishment. Over and over, he would hear the sound of Mistress Talia, as she would put the poor woman through her paces, listening to the woman scream over and over again, whimpering, crying and begging for the torture to stop. And David would be secure in his little cell, almost secure in the fact that it appeared no one was going to torture him because he had pretty much been abandoned by everyone. It was really weird, but he was experiencing the strange paradigm of listening to a woman being tortured right next door to him, but he was suffering in no way other than an inability to do anything for himself and an inability to have an erection. Granted, both of these problems were not fun by any stretch of the imagination, but David also got the impression that he was getting off far easier than that poor girl.

And David had very little contact with anyone for that matter. Mistress Cynthia might visit a few times a day to either feed him, spray him with a hose (in the cell itself) or to check to make sure he hadn't managed to slip out of his chastity belt in any way. The funny thing was, at least to David at the time, was that Mistress Cynthia appeared to have little care for anything concerning David other than her vigilant check to make sure that he did not gain an erection, or goddess forbid, succeed in obtaining an ejaculation. But Mistress Cynthia was very good at making sure such a contingency never happened, so David was left alone, pondering his slavery for hours with nothing to do or anyone to speak to.

In the beginning, during the first day or so of this process, it was slightly exciting, even though David couldn't do make use of that excitement without more pain for allowing himself to start growing an erection. It is very hard to describe the pain involved when one is in a chastity device, but this one device was designed to keep one's penis both bent and very small. Once a cock began to grow, the device would not expand with the cock and would immediately shut down any growth the body wanted to obtain. As such, the blood had no other place to go, and the swelling would pretty much incapacitate a man for a time period until the desire for an erection finally diminished. If David was living alone and not completely sexually stimulated every moment of the day, it would have been fine, but being locked in a cage in harnessed bondage, it was very hard to not think about the whole thing as exciting, and it only served to cause him more and more frustration and discomfort. And sadly enough, that only served to excite him more. It was one of those ironic situations that one cannot possibly describe because no one can ever imagine a sensation as well as one might have to live the experience. Even David imagined being put through such a torture in his many fantasies, but this was definitely not something he wanted to have to maintain on a constant basis, and that, unfortunately, is where many fantasies fail to live up to the reality; at least in a fantasy, the fantasizer has the ability to relieve himself once the fantasy has succeeded in exciting him enough. Not the same for reality.

David, even though it was a frustrating experience, actually found himself more interested in the perils of the young woman in the next cell. He had no idea what was actually happening to her, but he certainly did not think that it was something he would have wanted to experience. He knew all about Mistress Talia, and it was not just her playful desire to dominate him that he feared in the past. He knew she was cruel. Men who had served her in the past talked about her as a serious dominatrix who knew no mercy towards her slaves, and although he had no first-hand knowledge of this, it was believed that two men she had taken as personal slaves had given up the desire to submit completely after having been put through hell by her. One of them moved across the country and even changed his phone number so she might not ever find him again. Well, that was the story he heard from the other women at Mistress Dominique's house back then, but there was never any way to know what was contrived for the image and what was actually true.

However, he did remember one day when he was vacuuming the upstairs dungeon for Mistress Dominique, and he had pretty much been left alone in the house as it was after session hours. David did his usual job of cleaning to the best of his abilities. He was naked, like always, and he was beyond the stage of where he used to masturbate without permission, so he was pretty much doing exactly what he was supposed to do when he realized that there was someone standing behind him. He turned off the vacuum cleaner and turned around, seeing Mistress Talia standing in the doorway with her hands on her hips.

It was no secret that David had a thing for Mistress Talia. She was an extremely beautiful Chinese woman with long black hair with what could only be described as a body to die for. She knew men craved her attention, and she never failed to take complete advantage of the way that they looked at her. Men and women had a tendency to take her for granted, seeing her as the beautiful, mousy Asian girl who could easily fill the fantasy of any man seeking out an Asian school-girl. She was just that cute. But it was that tendency to take her for granted that proved to be the undoing of everyone who stepped into her spider web of control. In moments, she would transform from the cutest little girl who ever lived into the Bitch From Hell Who Knows No Mercy, and she would do it so fast that her victims would still think she was the cutest little girl who ever lived but somehow they had stepped into Bizarro World.

And Mistress Talia was not beyond using her cute, beautiful and cunning ways to get exactly what she wanted, even if it was never obvious exactly what it was she wanted. On this day, she stood in the doorway of the upstairs dungeon, and she was dressed in a one-piece latex suit that hugged her body from toe to the low cut top of it that accentuated her very sought after features. She wore red and black boots, and there was a riding crop resting in her right hand, its end slowly being tapped against the palm of her gloved left hand. "Where is Mistress Dominique?" said Mistress Talia.

David took a deep breath before speaking. He always had a hard time speaking around Mistress Talia. "Mistress, she went shopping. I'm not sure when she'll be back."

She glanced around the room. "Are you about done here?"

David wasn't sure what to say. Yes, he was about done with

the vacuuming, which meant that he was then required to head down to the basement and wait in the main dungeon outside of the cage until Mistress Dominique returned home. This was pretty much how every day of his was spent since becoming full-time houseboy. But he honestly did not know if it was wise to tell Mistress Talia that he was finished with his required tasks for the evening.

Finally, he spoke. "Yes, Mistress. I am finished."

She just smiled and shook her head. "Boy, are you ever going to regret that you answered yes." She then walked into the room and started walking around him, grabbing the handle of the vacuum cleaner from him and tossing it aside so that he was holding nothing in his hands. "You know, you're not like the other houseboys that Mistress Dominique has had here in the past. You know that, don't you?"

David wasn't exactly sure what she meant by the question. But he also knew that she expected an answer, and he was about to give one when she continued, cutting him off from what he was about to say. "No, you haven't any idea what I'm talking about, do you?"

She circled around him again. "On your knees, slave. Don't make me feel like you think you might be my equal."

Quickly, he dropped to his knees.

"That's the way slaves should always be: naked and on their knees. Spread your legs wider." He did. "You seem to have this problem here that I'm beginning to believe you don't even realize." She continued walking around him, circling him over and over in very slow movement. "We have had many houseboys here before, but you're the first one that Mistress Dominique has kind of put off limits to the rest of the girls."

David didn't know what she meant because if he was off limits, they sure did a lot of on limit stuff to him that didn't make sense.

"Did you know that Mistress Dominique once saved you from me?"

David followed her, making circles with his head as she walked around him. He was sure she wanted him to keep eye contact with her because she seemed to relish making it with him. "No, Mistress. I did not."

She nodded her head yes and then stopped walking. "A few months ago. I was kind of on the warpath, looking for someone to take down big time, and luck would have it, you showed up for your regular duties at the house. I told Mistress Dominique, I was going to take you upstairs to the bedroom, tie you face down to the bed and fuck you all night long. I was going to stay here throughout the night and just keep taking you over and over again." She smiled and then continued walking around him again. "I notice that doesn't scare you." She glanced at his cock that was hardening really fast-like. "It even seems to excite you. Well, let me just tell you that it would have been the worst experience of your life because in every fantasy that you have where it would be pleasurable, I promise you that I would have made it painful and unbearable. You would have been screaming throughout the entire night, and if it weren't screaming that brought me pleasure, I would find other ways to torture you until you pretty much either passed out, died or became putty in my hands. And two out of the three wouldn't have bothered me either."

David thought about the situation for a moment. Yes, it probably would have been horrible, but he couldn't help but be excited by the possibility. Mistress Talia was probably one of the most beautiful women he had ever come to know, even if she had a tendency to hate his guts and possibly everything he ever stood for.

"But Mistress Dominique saved you. You probably remember that day pretty well. Mistress Dominique told you to go home, that she wasn't feeling well." Mistress Talia started to laugh. "She faked being sick just to keep me from fucking you all night long."

David remembered that day. At the time, he thought he had displeased Mistress Dominique because during that period she tended to confide in him when things weren't going so hot for her, and he pretty much served as her sounding board (or at least one of them), so this came as a complete surprise to him. He figured she was mad at him, and he worked even harder than before the next time he showed up because he was convinced she was going to dump him and find another houseboy.

"You didn't know, did you?" said Mistress Talia.

"No, Mistress," said David.

She started to run her fingers through his hair. "Yep, I had tons of plans for you that night. Instead, Mistress Dominique called up some guy that used to be a houseboy for her and pretty much sacrificed him to the evil Mistress Talia. Poor guy didn't even know what was coming. But Mistress Dominique honestly thought I hadn't figured out what she had done. But I did."

David started to wonder if Mistress Talia was drunk because

this was the most conversation she'd ever had with him in all the time he had known her, especially considering it was conversation that didn't serve to allow her to demean him in some way, something she seemed to take great pleasure in doing so.

"I know you wanted to serve me a long time ago," she said. Then she stopped running her hands through his hair. He was waiting for her to say something to add to what she just said, but for some reason, she went silent for a long time. Then she spoke again. "Your status here is quickly changing. I don't know if you know this, and quite possibly it is not my place to say this, but in a very short time you may no longer be Mistress Dominique's houseboy."

David listened intently. This was the first he had heard about losing his status as Mistress Dominique's houseboy, or the possibility of losing that status. He knew his place, but he could not resist speaking. "Forgive me for asking, Mistress, but have I displeased Mistress Dominique in any way?"

Mistress Talia just started laughing and the laugh went on for a long time before she finally spoke again. "That's so like you. No, David, you have not displeased her in any way. As a matter of fact, I believe, having known Mistress Dominique as long as I have known her that you are probably going to become her personal slave before you realize it. If you're up to it, that is."

David's face lit up.

Her smile disappeared immediately. "I don't think you truly understand what that means. Believe me, you haven't fantasized anything that will meet with the reality of what you will experience if you become what she desires as her permanent slave."

David wasn't even listening anymore. Just the thought of becoming Mistress Dominique's personal slave was such a wonderful prospect. And then David suddenly began to question something that probably should have come to mind earlier during this conversation. Why was Mistress Talia telling him all of this?

She stopped moving and stared directly at him. "Very soon, you are going to be an owned slave. And you won't be mine either. You'll belong to Mistress Dominique." She walked towards the door. "Put away the vacuum and then meet me upstairs in the interrogation room."

David nearly swallowed his tongue. Granted, he had no idea what Mistress Talia had in mind for him, but just the possibility of finally serving her once was such a wonderful prospect. And if she were right about him becoming Mistress Dominique's permanent slave, the days of being the accessible houseboy would soon come to an end. While he would relish the possibility of finally being Mistress Dominique's slave, he had a feeling he would miss the interactions he seemed to have with most of the women who worked for and with his future owner.

After putting the vacuum away in the cleaning closet, he ran up to the interrogation room and then dropped to his knees in the center of the room. He found himself shaking, and he was starting to perspire. He was so excited it was unbelievable, and he was also scared to death. There was no doubt in his mind that Mistress Talia was in a league way out of the stratosphere of his own life's experience, so he was convinced virtually anything might happen.

A few minutes later, Mistress Talia came walking up the stairway, and he could hear her boots as they walked across the floor to the interrogation room. His eyes were forward, away from the door, so he didn't see her when she came in, but he knew she was there, and he heard her close the door behind him. Then she walked in front of him and stood for a moment, staring down into the eyes of the kneeling slave. It looked like she was going to say something, but she grabbed his right wrist shackle instead and led him to the far side of the room where there was a medieval-styled bench that served to drape a submissive over it either on his front or back with a wooden bar being used to support the body while there were hooks on both sides of the bar close to the floor. The purpose of the device was to push a submissive over the bar and then to lock him up so that he was resting on his stomach or back but completely exposed to the mistress about to torture him. The contraption was built low to the ground so that the slave was usually easily accessible to the mistress if she desired to spank, paddle or fuck him depending on her mood. However, for each of these circumstances, it required that the slave be tied up face down with his stomach resting on the device. David assumed as she led his right wrist to the hook at the base of the device that she was probably going to make good on her promise to fuck him.

But after she locked his right wrist manacle into the hook at the base, she turned him over so he was no longer lying on his stomach over the wooden bar. Instead, he was facing upwards, resting on his back. Then she proceeded to lock in his other wrist to the base so both of his arms were locked behind him in what was definitely uncomfortable but not impossible to maintain.

David was a bit unsure of what was about to happen here, and then she came up beside him and kicked both of his feet so that they were forced under the bar, with him falling back down to his knees. Then she proceeded to lock him in with his ankles pretty close to where his ankles were.

It was extremely uncomfortable, but the best way to describe it was David was tied up so that he was facing up, his head exposed and his cock pretty close to the base of the torture device. Without saying a word, Mistress Talia grabbed a rope from a hook on the wall, of which there was a huge selection of ropes and bondage equipment in this room, which made sense as this was called the Interrogation Room, and it would need such items to fill up such a named room. Mistress Talia took the rope and tied it around the base of his cock, and then she pulled it so that she was pulling his cock under the wooden bar, and behind his body. She pulled until his cock practically disappeared under him, or behind him, and then she tied off the rope to a hook located somewhere near where his hands and ankles were locked down. It was extremely uncomfortable.

Then Mistress Talia walked around the bondage device and stepped right up to his face. He realized right then and there that he was tied up in a position that essentially stuck his face right into her crotch, even though his head was slightly arched back due to the way she had put him into bondage.

"Mistress Dominique will not be back for awhile," said Mistress Talia. "She called earlier to let me know. You might even say that she's slightly responsible for what is going to happen here."

David started to wonder what was going to happen here. He was tied up in a way that didn't make it seem like she was going to fuck him, unless she was going to stick a dildo down his mouth, or something like that. She had complete access to his cock from this position, but something told him that that was too simple. That was not what was about to happen here.

"David, this is the only time this will ever happen, so you are to do your very best and remember the treasure you are getting here today. The next time you see me, understand that you will suffer horrendously because very few men will ever get this opportunity with me. So I advise you to steer clear of me from this day forward, or you will suffer the consequences. Do you understand me?"

"Yes, Mistress," said David, even though he didn't exactly understand what was about to happen.

Then Mistress Talia reached behind her and unzipped the jumpsuit she was wearing, the whole outfit falling to the floor as she did so. She slipped out of her boots and then pulled off what was left of the latex jumpsuit.

David knew she was beautiful, but this was something he never expected. Of all the women that worked at the house, he had seen sporadic moments of flesh from Mistress Talia, but he always got the idea that she did not like being naked around him for some reason, even though she probably had no qualms about nudity in her regular sessions as she was quite known in the scene for exposing her beautiful body as yet another means of frustrating submissives.

Then she did the unthinkable. Naked, she walked over to him and then forced her body onto his face and said only one thing: "Make me cum, and do it well."

Surprisingly, David rarely saw Mistress Talia after that. For the most part, he had done a pretty good job avoiding her whenever possible during the times before this incident, so it was not that much of a shock when he did not see her that much after. A few times he would run across her, and she would be her usual mean self and he would then do everything to avoid her again. Some things, no matter how certain actions would suggest otherwise, tend to never change.

One time, when the two of them happened to be alone in the house, and it appeared that he was definitely going to become Mistress Dominique's slave and that his interactions with the rest of the women was discouraged by Mistress Dominique more and more, Mistress Talia had David massage her feet, much like the very first time when he had first come to be a houseboy at the establishment. She said very little, but the one thing she said that never escaped his memory was that if she ever had the opportunity to put him under her spell again, whether from permission by Mistress Dominique or through the random circumstances of the universe, she would make him suffer like he's never suffered before. It seemed so out of context considering the one intimate moment they shared, but she gave him a look at the time that told him she was most serious, and that if he were ever unlucky enough to cross paths with her again, he would most certainly be the one to suffer.

So, when David found himself in the cell, hearing the voice of Mistress Talia, he couldn't help but feel a bit of terror every time he heard a boot walking down the corridor, convinced it was Mistress Talia coming for him. One time, he heard those boots walking towards his cell, and he heard the sound of the cell door opening, and he awaited the inevitable scream-inducing pain she was about to cause. Then he heard the voice of Mistress Cynthia, and he breathed a sigh of relief. And then Mistress Cynthia beat the crap out of him, possibly out of just a desire to do so or because she recognized that he was actually relieved to have her appear in his cell, and some things, like fear, really need to be reinforced.

Chapter XVIII

David used to hear stories about prisoners forced into solitary confinement, and sometimes such events were dramatized on television, and he always imagined that it wouldn't be that bad. As a matter of fact, under the circumstances, he figured it would probably be pretty enjoyable. After all, beautiful women keeping men locked in solitary confinement in bondage with the threat of beatings. How could it not be enjoyable?

Well, it was another one of those "fantasy is so much better than damn reality" situations. Whenever he saw such actions depicted in movies or on television, it was usually for a day or two, the prisoner was usually locked in a cage alone and naked, and the stir crazy effect usually ended up breaking the prisoner and the release at the end of the ordeal was usually such a great moment for the prisoner. But this was usually over the course of a few days at the most, and while the prisoner was usually kept naked, the prisoner was rarely tied up, placed into a male chastity device, fed gruel or nothing at all and then beaten in the middle of the night (or day as it was practically impossible to know the difference under such circumstances). In the dramatized version of this kind of prison situation, there was usually something that caused the solitary confinement, and the prisoner was almost always shown as combative towards his captors. In David's situation, he was put into solitary confinement because it was something that pleased Mistress Cynthia, and unlike the prisoners he'd seen in movies and television, there was nothing David could do to avoid the punishment that he was receiving.

David was in solitary for a few days before he started to get a grasp on the routine. While he could hear the sounds of the poor woman being tortured over and over, he began to feel a bit of comfort in the fact that Mistress Talia never seemed to notice that he was in the next cell. He didn't actually know if this was the case, that she had no idea he was there, but it felt so much better thinking that she was going on with her daily life without realizing he was quite possibly right under her thumb and close enough for her to do whatever it is she might feel like doing.

Then again, if David was lucky, maybe Mistress Talia didn't even remember who he was. It had been a few years since he last saw her, although he always assumed that she had found a house somewhere else and was torturing a whole new group of slaves during professional sessions. Of course, David had noticed at one point that Mistress Talia appeared to have disappeared off the radar screen of session dominants, not appearing in any major magazines or movies as most of the hotter dominants appeared to be doing once gaining a reputation in the scene. He had figured at some point that she had probably grown tired of doing professional sessions and went back to a vanilla life, or she had found some very rich submissive who made it so that she never had to work again.

That last possibility was the one David always imagined happened, but common sense used to bite at him back then telling him that would never happen. Mistress Talia took great pleasure in torturing slaves; this was not the kind of woman who would turn away from potential victims easily.

However, this kind of place was definitely not where David expected to run into Mistress Talia. As a matter of fact, this kind of a place was not where David expected to run into David either, but that pretty much went without saying.

During those first few days of solitary confinement, David did notice that there was a pattern to the way things were happening. While he had no idea what time it was, or even what part of the day it might be, he was usually guaranteed a visit from Mistress Cynthia who would check that chastity device, spray him with water, feed him and then possibly whip him just because he was there. It was rarely punishment because he had done something wrong, but the kind of punishment that a woman would inflict just because she had access to a subdued naked man who had no way to resist, nowhere to escape to, and no one's ear to listen to him if he tried to complain. For Mistress Cynthia, it was a wonderful situation; for David, it was a life he was forced to live, and like it or not, that was just the way it was going to be.

It was a few days into his solitary confinement, or at least what he believed to be a few days, when David realized that it had been a long time since Mistress Cynthia last showed up. He could always tell when she was past due depending on how many times he used the toilet in the corner of the cell. Two times of relieving himself was usually about the time it took for her to return and remind him that he wasn't on some sort of vacation but that he was a slave being punished by a woman who took great pleasure in punishing him.

But as he relieved himself for the fourth time, he began to realize that it had been a long time since she last showed up. He heard the sounds of boots walking down the corridor outside his cell a few times, but he could never be sure that it was her, and he knew better than to make a sound to attract a woman's attention in this place. While Mistress Cynthia would surely punish him for making unauthorized noise, he had no clue what would happen if the person who heard him happened to be Mistress Talia; not only did he not know how she would handle such a situation, he also knew that if she realized who he was, what might happen to him might be far worse than anything else that might happen instead.

Realizing he was all alone and that it was quite possible that he was going to be all alone for a very long time, he began to try to figure out the general layout of this cell that he was being kept in. The furnishings really didn't take that much time to figure out, as the only thing he had come across in the room was one toilet in the far corner. Aside from him, the place was completely empty.

The floor felt like it was made of stone, and it had that cold stone feel to it. The walls appeared to be made of a similar substance as well. As he ran his fingers across the surface of the wall from his hands that were locked behind his back, he was convinced that it had to be some kind of heavy stone that made up the wall of this place. It was obvious that if someone was trying to escape, going through the wall was not going to be a possibility.

That left the door. When he was first locked in the cell, he imagined the door was a cage with bars going across it, but when he listened to the sound of boots outside the cell, he realized he was listening to slightly muffled footfalls which indicated that the door was of thickness, not open with bars blocking his exit. One evening, when he was restless, he maneuvered his way over to the door and felt the door with his hands, realizing for the first time that the door was constructed of metal. Running his hands alongside the bottom of the door, he felt a small open area but noticed that there was some kind of bar structure going across that area as well. That was when he realized there was some kind of trap door at the bottom of the massive door itself, possibly a place where food was set into the cell so that the mistress would not have to go through the work of opening the whole door just to feed a slave. It was while he was trying to get more of a feel for the substance of this door that he realized his mistake. Like most cell doors, they are not designed to be pushed over and over without making a sound. And that was exactly what happened. He was making a sound as the door moved less than an inch each time he tried to feel its substance. The lock on the door itself kept the cell door from opening and allowing him freedom, but the fact that it had that lock on it kept the door in movement over and over so that it was making a clanging sound each time he pressed against it.

That was when he heard the sound of Mistress Talia. "Slave, what the hell are you doing over there?"

The voice was coming from some distance down the corridor, but the sound of boots running towards his cell immediately told him that he was about to get a visit from his former nemesis. She was running down the corridor to his cell, in HER PRISON.

David quickly backed up to the other side of the cell and tried to act like he had been doing nothing wrong, although he knew that such an attempt was probably not going to do him much good in this place. "Probable cause" didn't really seem to be a concept germane to this place.

He heard those boots stop right outside of his cell and then dead silence. For a long time.

David took a deep breath and held it in, not about to make the mistake of saying a single thing that might make her think it was necessary to enter this cell. Yet, all he could hear outside of his cell was silence.

It seemed to go on forever. He knew she was right there, just listening, and he knew that anything he did would make noise, so he found himself forced to remain completely still, yet cognizant of every tiny sound he made, including breathing and his chest moving in and out. At one point, he actually felt he could hear the sound of sweat pouring from his skin as he became more and more terrified over what was going to happen in the next few moments.

Then he heard the sound of her boots as she started to slowly walk back in the direction in which she had come. He heard one boot fall and then another, and then…nothing. More silence.

Then he heard a sound he had hoped he would not hear. It was laughter, that very familiar laugh that could only come from Mistress

Talia.

"Do you really think you can fool me, slave?" she said. "Did you think you could try to get out of your cage and not have your jailor know you were trying to escape?"

Escape? David wanted to blurt out that that was the last thing in the world he was trying to do, but an accidental burst of common sense held his tongue.

Then he heard those boots as they closed the distance again. Now, she was standing in front of the cell's door, his cell's door. He held his breath until he heard the sound he was hoping he would not hear, the sound of keys turning in the door's lock. Then he heard the sound as the cell door swung open. And then the sound of those boots as they entered his cell.

He listened intently and made no attempt to move as she closed the distance to where he was on the other side of the cell. What seemed like a huge distance to him while he was tied up in this box, she crossed it in mere moments. Then he felt her boot as it came down from above and rested on his left shoulder. "Slave, you have no idea what you have gotten yourself into."

David believed he knew a little more than she suspected; he just didn't know if she knew who he was.

"I am the jailor here," she said with almost a laugh as she spoke. Then her tone turned serious and menacing again. "That means that anything that happens here to you is a result of how I decide it should happen. I assume you've been listening to the fun I've been inflicting on Mary Ann." She grabbed his hood and pulled back his head so that if he had been able to see through the hood, he would have been staring back up at her. "If I ask you a question here, I don't want an answer from you. I noticed you were about to answer; I could really care less what you have to say." She then released his head and rested her boot on his shoulder again. "I guess you could say that I am someone who experiences great job satisfaction."

David began to wonder if this was a familiar theme as it was something he'd heard a number of times.

"You poor man," she said. "A chastity tube on you and no way to even get an erection. It must really suck to be you."

This was one definite point David wasn't about to argue.

"How's this, slave? How about we give you a little fun instead of so much pain and discomfort?"

David didn't like the direction this was heading. These women didn't know the meaning of fun, at least not so that he felt like he was experiencing it. But he didn't exactly have much of a choice either.

"Mary Ann is tied up and exposed, just waiting for me to go back and do something evil to her. Only, I can't decide whether I want to bullwhip her until she's bleeding all over the place or whether I might want to violate every orifice she has over and over again until she's bleeding that way as well. How about you decide for me? From this moment on, you get to decide how Mary Ann suffers."

This was definitely not something that sounded like fun to David. He hated to see a woman suffer, and he certainly didn't want to be the one who decided how she would suffer, especially when those two choices were the only options.

"What I want you to do is lie down and then role over onto your left if you want her to be bullwhipped or role over to your right if you'd rather she be fucked everywhere possible."

David didn't know what to do.

"You don't have a choice," said Mistress Talia. "You either must choose."

David decided that whatever punishment she wanted to inflict on him would be fine. He just didn't want to make that decision.

She started to laugh again. "There is no easy way out of this, slave. If you choose not to choose, I will do both of those things to her, and you will be the one who condemned her to that."

David thought quickly. He realized he had to choose one or the other, or both. For an instant, he actually thought of not choosing because he realized that this woman was eventually going to be one of them, and the chances were pretty good that she was probably going to be torturing him one day, and she would probably take great pleasure in doing so.

But then he realized he couldn't rely on that as the criteria for his decision so he analyzed it quickly and realized that at least one of those circumstances offered her a chance of pleasure along with the pain. So he rolled over to his right.

Mistress Talia said nothing for a moment before she walked back out of the cell and then locked the door behind her. He could then hear her boots as she walked down the corridor to wherever it was the other slave was located. He could hear everything.

"Mary Ann," said Mistress Talia, loud enough so there was no way David could not hear her. "Get the fuck up! It's time for me to fuck you."

"No, Mistress," said the whimpering voice of Mary Anne, "please, not again!"

"Silence, slave," said Mistress Talia. "Let's just say that this pleasure you are about to receive comes from the slave in the next cell. He asked me to fuck you up the ass."

That wasn't how it went, thought David. But then he also realized he had no word in the conversation, so that was how it was going to be.

"That son of a bitch!" she said. "I'll fucking skin him alive once I get out of here!"

He could hear Mistress Talia's laugh again. "You first have to get through me, Missy. That might take a lot of time."

"I'll wait," she said. "He's fucking dead when this is all over."

"That's enough speaking, Mary Ann. I demand silence from this moment forward. We have a little penetrating to do here, and I really need my concentration." There was a slight pause. "Do not move. I'll be right back with all the fun in the world. Too bad you won't enjoy it as much as I will."

Then David heard the sound of the cage door slam shut down the hall and the sound of Mistress Talia's boots as she came closer to his cell. Then he heard the sound of what appeared to be a trap being opened on his own cell door and then Mistress Talia speaking in almost a whisper so that only he could hear. "Welcome to Hell, slave. You don't even have a clue what you've gotten yourself into."

David was beginning to hear that more and more these days. It was coming true more and more as well.

Chapter XIX

Throughout that night, David could hear the screams of that poor woman, but all he could focus on was the fact that woman was probably blaming him for what was happening to her. He would think she would have to know he would have no ability to make a decision like that about what was going to happen to her, but then he also realized that when someone is in such a state of slavery and is being tortured constantly, one doesn't really give it a lot of thought but essentially goes with whatever is being represented to him or her. As it was, Mary Ann, a future dominant in this place, now considered David someone who would be owed a great deal of retribution, and he had no doubt that when it came time for her to find out who it was she needed to seek out for that vengeance, Mistress Talia would go out of her way to release that information to her, even though there was a pretty good chance that Mistress Talia had no idea who David was at this particular moment.

The fact that Mistress Talia might not realize he was here was still very much a fear for David. He had no idea how she would react, but an inner feeling told him that it would probably not go very well for him. Judging from the short conversation he had with her in his cell, well, the conversation she had with him to be more precise, he realized she was no different than she was before, and quite possibly she was even meaner than she was back then. He was getting the impression that she had a lot of experience in causing distress and pain since they last met. Unfortunately, David couldn't claim an equal amount of experience in taking distress and pain during that period of time, so like always, she was completely at an advantage.

But surprisingly, the prospect of Mistress Talia knowing who he was seemed of little importance to David. A few days had passed since Mistress Talia had spoke to him in his cell, and David was beginning to get really thirsty and hungry. He realized he hadn't seen Mistress Cynthia in quite some time.

Had she completely forgotten about him? That didn't seem possible. She had spent so much time with him that he couldn't imagine that she had forgotten him.

Then strange thoughts started to run through his head. What if something happened to Mistress Cynthia? The chances were pretty good that she didn't live in this place; at least such a probability made sense, as this was Mistress Dominique's place. What if something happened to Mistress Cynthia while she was away from the place doing whatever it was she did when she wasn't here torturing David? Would anyone even know that she was gone? Did she punch a time clock, or did she just show up when she felt it was appropriate? If it was the latter of the two circumstances, David began to realize that no one would even know if he'd been taken care of while in this place. They might just assume that Mistress Cynthia was okay, and therefore, so was he.

Would they let him starve to death because they didn't even know something was wrong?

What if Mistress Cynthia just quit and didn't tell anyone? He didn't believe that could have happened, but it was always a possibility. Mistress Cynthia obviously didn't have the same rules keeping her here that kept David here. He wondered if she could be as cruel as to just leave and not tell anyone that the slave was locked in solitary confinement, possibly never to be seen again.

David was about to try figuring out how to get water out of the toilet, even though it wouldn't be easy with his hands locked behind his back when he heard a sound that went beyond beautiful music. It was the sound of heels walking down the corridor, heading towards his cage. He didn't know if he was going to be punished, chastised or what, but it had been some time since anyone spoke to him, and he was willing to accept anything.

The heels stopped right outside of his cell, and he waited to hear the sound of keys in the lock, but that's not what happened. Instead, he heard the sound of the food trap of the door as the aperture was pulled open and something plopped onto the floor of his cell. Then the aperture was pulled shut again, and then silence again. After a few moments, the heels started moving down the corridor again.

The person who came to his cell didn't say a word. The one thing he had been looking forward to disappeared just as soon as it had appeared. He was left with as much silence as he had before.

Slowly, David dragged himself over to the cell door, being careful not to knock over whatever it was that was dropped into his cell, especially if it was something to drink. He didn't want to end up losing his only drink by being foolish and knocking it over. Even though he probably wouldn't last very much longer, he doubted Mistress Cynthia would give him more if it were his fault for losing what she had already given him. This kind of slavery was strange that way.

It was a jug of pretty large size, and as David managed to get it into his hands, he realized that it was like a water bottle with a tip one could bite to cause the water to release. It was sort of like a very large baby bottle, although David assumed this bottle was probably one of the kinds he had seen bicyclers using on long distance trips.

Biting onto the nipple of the bottle, David took in some of the liquid. His first reaction was that this wasn't water as it tasted a bit tangier than water. He thought quickly and then hoped it wasn't what he thought it might be. But he was so thirsty, he was willing to drink whatever it was they had given him. He went through nearly half the bottle before he no longer felt the pangs of thirst upon him.

He didn't know what he had been drinking, but he was beyond the point of really caring. He was willing to do whatever he had to do to survive this place, even if it meant drinking piss, something he had never done before, and something he never intended to try if it would have been up to him.

Unfortunately for him, very little was up to him these days.

Days passed. No one visited David anymore. Every now and then, the cell's door trap door would open and some food or liquid would be placed into the cell. One time, the door opened, and some-one came into the cell, but all the person did was tug on his chastity device a few times to make sure it was secure and then grab the few bottles that had been gathering in the cell with David. Whoever it was that came into the room said nothing at all and almost seemed to pay zero attention to David, except for the checking of the chastity device. David wondered if anyone was ever going to speak to him again.

A few days further into this and David was going stir crazy. He finally understood what those movies about prison solitary confine-ment were about. When this "adventure" had begun, there had been enough conversation from either Mistress Cynthia and the one time from Mistress Talia. Other times, he could hear the poor whimper-ing girl elsewhere in the complex, and quite often he could hear her being tortured, so there was always something that would activate his senses.

However, after the one time that Mistress Talia came into his cell, there was nothing. He no longer heard the poor girl whimpering or suffering. Mistress Talia never reappeared, and Mistress Cynthia seemed to be on some kind of vacation from him.

David never realized how much the human mind craved sound from others and other things. Even the few times he heard boots on the floor outside were moments to relish. However, he began to believe that the women walking outside his cell were no longer wearing boots or heeled shoes. He was beginning to suspect they were wearing either socks or going bare foot because he no longer heard anything. The last time he heard the trap door open to drop off liquid, he swore he never heard the sound of feet, as they had to have crossed the stone floor to his cell. It was as if they were doing everything possible to make sure that he heard nothing.

He had no idea how long it had been. He just knew that he was extremely lonely, and he wanted to talk to someone, to listen to someone talk to him, even if it was to have someone scold him for an hour about things he did or did not do. He needed some type of stimulation of any type.

His mind started to wander more and more. In the beginning, the time to think was wonderful, and he allowed his imagination to roam freely, but after days of doing nothing but think, he found it almost painful to think. He would start thinking of something and then realize that all he could hear was his own mind, and it was almost like an echo of loneliness was constantly overwhelming him.

He had no idea how long it had been since Mistress Cynthia first put him into this cell. He tried to guess and figured it had been a week and a half, but he had no way of really knowing for sure. He just knew he hated it more than anything.

That was until he heard the obvious sound of boots walking down the corridor towards his cell. The boots stopped right in front of the door, and he waited to hear the trap door open so he would have either liquid or a miniscule amount of food, but instead he heard the sound of the keys as they opened the cell's door itself.

As much as he had been looking forward to a visit from anyone, he now found himself shaking in fear. It had been awhile, and he had no idea what was going to happen next.

The sound of boots could be heard as they walked into his cell. Then the walking stopped. Whoever it was who entered his cell was standing right inside the entrance. He imagined the woman was probably just staring at him, waiting for him to do something stupid.

Then he heard her laugh. It was the laugh of Mistress Cynthia.

"You are a pathetic sight, do you know that, slave?"

He made no attempt to answer her through the hood. That was one of those questions she tended to ask not expecting an answer.

"I'll bet you don't have a clue how long you've been in here, do you?"

He hoped it was two weeks, the time she condemned him to. He shook his head no.

The laugh started up again. "Would you believe it's only been four days?"

No, he would not believe that. He knew it had to be well over a week. There was no doubt in his mind. That was when it hit him.

The time could be however long she decided it was.

"Four days, slave. You're not even halfway through the horror of this place."

A wave of desperation came over him much like a sense of heat. He knew he couldn't stand another period of time in this place alone. He just wasn't cut out for this kind of thing.

"If it's only been four days, I'll bet you're wondering why I'm here talking to you now."

That thought never actually crossed his mind. He was just glad to hear her voice.

"This may surprise you, but I'm here to apologize to you."

Okay, this didn't seem to make any sense. It certainly didn't belong in this atmosphere of women who tortured men with careless abandon.

"Yes, I'm here to apologize," she said. "When I condemned you to this place, I made certain promises to you, and I forgot to deliver. I guess I was too wrapped up in some aspects of your imprisonment that I forgot the rest."

He was confused.

"Do you remember what I promised you if you cried out back then when I was torturing you?"

He thought quickly. It was all a haze.

The boots started walking again, and they came right over to him. Then he felt her tugging at his hood, pulling at a Velcro fastener that was over his mouth and then he felt the zipper being pulled to a side, releasing his mouth for the first time in a long time.

He breathed in the stale air of the cell for the first time that was not filtered by the hood, and even though it was stale as would be expected from a prison cell in a dungeon, it was the sweetest air he remembered in a long time because all he could remember was the smell of that leather hood.

"Tell me, slave. What do you remember me threatening you with if you failed?"

David took a deep breath of that dungeon air and then tried to remember. "Mistress Cynthia, you told me that you would lock me up for two weeks in a chastity belt and I would be kept in complete bondage during that period."

She laughed again. "It's amazing how you conveniently forgot the most important promise I added as well. I also promised to put you through pain that you'd never been through before. You do remember that, don't you?"

David did but wished he had not. "Yes, Mistress Cynthia."

"Oh, what fun we'll have. And by the way, if I remember correctly, I also added a stipulation to the end of that offer: this would last until I was pleased you paid for your crime. That might be two weeks. That might be until the end of your pathetic life."

David hated this. No matter how hard he tried to work within the constraints of what they did to him, the rules always appeared to be changing on him.

"On your feet, slave," she said. "I wouldn't want you telling anyone that Mistress Cynthia is a woman that doesn't live up to her promises."

He tried to stand up, but he discovered nothing he did would work. He didn't even have the energy in his legs to rise up off the ground. His hands tied behind his back didn't help either.

She sighed. "You are so pissing me off, slave. Don't think that just because I promised you a vacation of two weeks in this place that it means you have to live until the end of that two weeks." She then reached down and pulled him to his feet. Then her voice turned almost cheerful, kind of giddy. "Come on, come on, lots of fun for us today." Then she pulled him behind her with her fingers through the ring in his collar.

David hobbled after her, realizing for the millionth time that he needed to stop wishing for things here because they always seemed to come true for him, and not once has the fulfilled wish ever been something he desired. For days and nights he wished for the solitude to end, and now that it was ending for a moment, he knew he was not going to enjoy what was going to be happening to him very soon.

She dragged him behind her for some distance until she came turned to the right and continued pulling him behind her. They never went up any stairs, so David realized they were still in the prison somewhere. However, when he heard Mistress Cynthia unlocking a door before them, he heard the sound of what had to be a huge door being moved to its side, indicating that this room she was leading him to was not your average sized cell. The door to this place made the next room appear much larger than the door to David's own cell ever did. Of course, he had no way of knowing if this conclusion was correct, but there didn't appear to be much of an attempt to mask these sorts of things here, so he didn't suspect this information was going to do him any good, nor that it was incorrect in any way.

Mistress Cynthia led him across the room and then forced him down to his knees. His knees landed on a large piece of wood, and he realized he was on some kind of frame of some sorts. She locked his ankles to rings on the wooden platform so that his legs were stretched far away from each other, exposing his lower body while he was on his knees. Then she pulled back on a chain she had placed between the restraints connecting his wrists together behind his back and then attached that chain to a lock close to where the ankle rings were located. He was left in a leaning back position, unable to move. Then, to remind him that she rarely forget anything, Mistress Cynthia zipped back up his hood and then reattached the Velcro fastener so that he would not be breathing through that aperture again.

While David knew to expect the unexpected from Mistress Cynthia, and he knew that he should be quite scared at this particular moment, it wasn't fear that was running his emotions this time. It was curiosity. He was curious like he'd never been before; he wanted to know what Mistress Cynthia had in store for him.

Then David felt the caress of a woman's hands as they ran across his naked chest slowly working their way down his body to his abdomen. Then they moved back up and then back down again. If he could have gotten hard, he would have been hard right then and there. He hated that chastity device more than anything. Well, at least for the moment. Who knew what he was going to end up hating two minutes later?

He felt a boot kick up against his cock's cage. He grimaced in discomfort, not exactly pain, but frustrated helplessness. "How long has he been wearing this thing?"

The voice was not Mistress Cynthia's. It was the voice of Mistress Talia.

"Since I brought him down here," she said.

It figures, thought David. Just when it looked like he was going to get information, like how long he had really been here, they still managed to keep that information from him.

"Take it off him," she said.

Then David felt a soft pair of hands as they maneuvered themselves around his crotch and unlocked the device that was stifling his erections. The moment it was off him, he felt a spasm of pain from all the blood expanding, and then without constraints to hold it back, his cock fully expanded.

To his surprise, David felt soft fingers as they ran themselves over his manhood for a few seconds and then abated. That one touch almost put him over.

"Not so fast," said Mistress Cynthia. "You come and it would upset Mistress Talia greatly. I don't think you want to do that."

"Think of Mistress Cynthia as good cop, and I'm bad cop," said Mistress Talia with a laugh. "But you know that already, don't you, David?"

David nearly swallowed his tongue. She knew who he was. And she apparently remembered him as well.

"You didn't think you could come into my prison without me knowing who you were, did you?" David had hoped it was going to work that way. "I never had such a hard time keeping it from you when you were making noise the other night. I wanted to tell you that your tormentor knew who you were, but I wanted to save that moment until today, when you would truly be under my spell."

David wasn't sure what that meant. Was Mistress Cynthia going to let Mistress Talia torture him for a while? Or what was happening?

David felt those soft fingers on his chest again. "David, our time together has come to an end. You have reached the next level of your slavery. Mistress Talia will train you from this point forward."

If the hood hadn't been covering his face, the two women would have seen David's eyes opening extremely wide. He had no desire to be trained by Mistress Talia. Well, that wasn't exactly true, but common sense told him that he would be a lot safer under the tutelage of Mistress Cynthia.

"Do you turn over all rights to this slave to me?" said Mistress Talia.

"Yes," she replied. "He is yours for the duration." Then David heard the sound of boots as Mistress Cynthia left the room and his life.

But it was not a time for good-byes.

"Slave, welcome to my prison," said Mistress Talia. "To be honest, I always knew this day would come. I just never realized how much enjoyment I would experience when it happened."

Chapter XX

David was pretty much resigned to accept whatever happened to him here, but this was a little different than what he expected. In the past, he had been subjected to all sorts of tortures and lifestyle adaptations that just seemed harsh and unfair. But that was all something he had signed onto as part of his understanding of what it would take to become Mistress Dominique's slave. So here he was, months later in the service of Mistress Dominique, and he had only seen her once, and he was now about to be in service to the one woman he had secretly craved since first coming into Mistress Dominique's life. The only thing that had ever saved him from her was the fact that Mistress Dominique was more interested in him than she was, and she had a certain say in his affairs that Mistress Talia never had. If it hadn't been for that fact, the chances were pretty good that David would have slowly fallen under Mistress Talia's spell back when he was just a houseboy, and he never would have become Mistress Dominique's slave. And now he was right back where he started, except it was Mistress Dominique who put him here.

It was all confusing.

He felt a tug at the straps on his hood and then realized that Mistress Talia was removing it from his head. It took her quite awhile to get the straps undone, but once she did, she pulled the contraption off of his head, and for the first time, he actually saw light. Dimly lit light, but light nonetheless. And that was when he saw her standing before him in all her beautiful glory.

She was more beautiful than he remembered from the last time he had seen her. She had disappeared from Mistress Dominique's house almost overnight, and it was only after some time that he realized she was not coming back, although no one ever told him she had quit, or she had left, or whatever had happened to her. He got the impression no one but Mistress Dominique ever really knew what had happened to her.

She was dressed in white, which was something he had never seen her wear before. It was a tight-fitting white equestrian outfit that hugged her body all over, and it was offset only by spit-shined boots that came all the way up to her knees. While David suspected that such an outfit was probably worn for the most part to turn on clients, he could also see that she felt completely comfortable in the outfit, and he knew there were probably not clients here that she needed to turn on in the first place.

The one thing that David noticed more than anything was her hair. Before, she had satin black hair that seemed pretty short and conservative. Now, that hair was flowing down to her mid back, and it was extremely beautiful on her. It was like she was someone completely different but just as, or more, beautiful than he last remembered seeing her.

"I'd say we have a lot of catching up to do, slave," she said, "but that wouldn't exactly be true. We never got a chance to start anything together. Mistress Dominique made that impossible."

David said nothing. He knew better than to say anything here, regardless of how much past they had between them.

"Isn't it ironic that the one woman who stuck a wedge between us is the one woman that brought us back together?"

Yes, David found that quite ironic. Kind of scary, actually.

"Okay, enough small talk," said Mistress Talia. "It's time to lay down some ground rules. Everything you were taught by Mistress Cynthia still stands. I expect complete obedience from you at all times, or I will punish you like you've never been punished before. I think you know me well enough to know that I'm not kidding here. It is important for you to completely understand your status here and to whom it is you serve. You are owned by Mistress Dominique, but through circumstances that are irrelevant, you are now owned by me. Until I am finished with you, you answer to me and you live your life for me. Is that understood?"

"Yes, Mistress," said David.

She stared at him for a very long time. "Hmm, you still have that interesting habit of calling me Mistress." She thought to herself for a moment. "Why is that? According to Mistress Cynthia, you refer to all the other women by their names and title, all except for Mistress Dominique. Why also me?"

David couldn't really explain it. "I'm not really sure, Mistress. It always just seemed natural, and you never told me to call you anything different."

She continued staring at him. "I've often wondered if there's something more to it than that. Either way, it's fine. I prefer it this way." She then started playing with his cock with her boot by softly kicking it from one side to another but not focusing direct attention on it so that it was more than just an annoyance with a bit of pleasure at the same time. It was obvious she wasn't intending to do it so that he'd cum but did it just to continue to frustrate him as his penis had been caged up for a very long time with zero stimulation. "I'm going to want a certain something from you, David, something that Mistress Cynthia never asked for." She stopped playing with his cock and them moved closer to him, so that her face was right in front of his. "I want you to give yourself over to me totally so that I am all that is important to you, so that I am all that exists in your world. You are to have no thoughts of anyone else: not an old girlfriend, not Mistress Cynthia, not Mistress Dominique, not anything but me. I am all you are to think about from this moment forward. If you have thoughts about other things, you are to quickly put them out of your mind, and if you find you cannot do that, you are to inform me immediately and then I will beat those things out of you until you come back to remembering the only thing that should be important to you. Do you understand this, slave?"

He thought quickly. "Yes, Mistress."

She stepped away from him. "No, you don't. You're just saying what you think I want to hear. If you understood what I wanted from you, you would be scared to death right now. For the first time, you'd actually try to figure out a way to escape out of this place, oblivious to any punishments you might receive for trying." She just stared at him. "Sometimes, you're hopeless."

She then walked to the other side of the room and pulled a whip from one of the many adorning the walls. It had a thick leather handle and straps of leather hanging from the end of it. It didn't appear very menacing, but David had been whipped many a time and knew that sort of whip could be very painful because it had a tendency to sting. He also noticed as she came closer with it that there were tiny balls at the end of the leather straps; that usually meant it was going to draw blood.

She draped the whip over his back and then balanced it on his shoulders by dropping the handle so it hung over his chest. She left it there and stepped back deeper into the darkness of this room that David was only now starting to observe for the first time as his eyes had cleared some, and he was getting the images in the dark of what this room consisted of.

It was a room of serious torture. There was no disguising that. He was on some kind of wooden platform that had stocks, although Mistress Cynthia had only locked him into the bottom portion of the piece of equipment proving that some bondage devices can have multiple purposes. There were cushioned tables with ratchet devices for stretching, some with the same purpose that had no cushions, racks on the wall, manacles on the wall, manacles on pulleys for hanging a slave from the ceiling, a wheel device that seemed to serve the purpose of tying a slave to one side of it and then turning him upside down over and over again. There were many other large pieces of equipment that he had no idea of how they were actually used, although his imagination was running wild. However, what was probably of more importance to David of all the items in this room was the whip that was hanging on him.

Mistress Talia stood before him. "You should remember that no session with me ever begins without a slave's body in flames first. The other mistresses might like comfortable slaves, but you need to suffer by my hand before we can move onto other things."

She then picked up the whip and immediately slashed it across what was exposed of his back from the position he was in. Then she continued to hit him in that general area over and over again until she drew blood. Then she moved onto another section of his back, continuing until she had the streak of blood from that area as well. Then she moved onto his front side and was whipping his arms, his chest and any exposed part of his body that she could reach. In only a few moments, David was in tears and in pain. But this only seemed to encourage her more.

She stopped at one point and smiled. "I'm sure most of your mistresses you've served tend to do warm-ups. Those serve two purposes: they get you ready to handle more, and they help you acclimate to the pain you're about to receive. That's for sessions. This is not a session. This is your real life. I could care less whether or not you are ready to handle more, and you will either acclimate to the pain as I inflict it upon you or you die. Either way is fine with me."

Then she proceeded to whip him, not stopping until he was sobbing and pretty much a basket case. This was about a half hour later.

Then she walked to another display of pain implements and

came back to him. She was holding a riding crop in her hands. "Looks good with the riding outfit, doesn't it?"

"Yes, Mistress," he said, quickly. It did look excellent and sexy, so he wasn't lying. He just wanted to make sure that she didn't punish him for hesitating concerning anything she wanted to hear from him.

"Of course it does," she said. "I'm a very beautiful woman, am I not?"

"Yes, Mistress," he said, still trying to recapture his breath from the whipping. "Yes, you are very beautiful."

"How beautiful, slave? Tell me how beautiful I am?"

He was never good at this kind of stuff. It always came out corny no matter how hard he tried to say it. "Mistress, you are quite possibly the most beautiful woman I have ever seen."

She frowned. "Possibly?"

He realized then that he shouldn't have quantified his statement with that adverb. "The most beautiful in the world, Mistress."

"Too late, slave. You need to learn that I am the only woman in your world right now. Not one of the best. The ONLY."

She then took the riding crop and took a step back, and then she brought it down with all her might across his penis. David screamed in pain. She stared at him for a second and then did the exact same thing again. David thrashed in his bonds from the pain, but he couldn't move at all. So Mistress Talia fired at him with the riding crop again, catching him on the other side of his cock this time.

David had been tortured many times before, but this was just straight out cruelty. And it continued. She then hit him across the balls, then a few more shots that came randomly in that area, and then back to his cock again. She hit him over and over again.

As David was suffering more and more, he noticed a very strange look on Mistress Talia's face. It was not anger or that look a woman gives when she's punishing a slave. It was something completely different. It was hard to even quantify. It looked like ecstasy on her face. He had never seen her with that expression on her face before except for the one time she had taken him at Mistress Dominique's house.

But his realization what was happening to Mistress Talia meant nothing because she continued doing it, hitting him over and over again. He had never known such pain before, at least not like this. But it wouldn't end either.

As she continued hitting him, she was laughing out loud, a sort of giddy laugh that comes when someone is having the time of her life. She was having such a good time of hitting him over and over again and causing so much pain to him that she didn't even notice that he had passed out on her.

When David woke up, he found himself still tied to the wood frame, and his penis and testicles were in serious pain. That torture wasn't something that just happened and then the pain went away. It was still painful; although it was not at the level of pain it had been while she was whipping him.

"You are such a wimp, David. I wasn't even halfway done with you when you passed out."

David was actually really scared now. He didn't want to go through that again. "Please, Mistress, that's way beyond what I can take."

She wiped her hands with a towel. "Excuse me, slave? At what point did you get the idea that you decide something is more than you can take?"

He said nothing.

"I decide what you can take and what you can't take. For instance, I think you can take what I just gave you even more than you already did. Do you dispute that, slave? Do you want to call me on that?"

"No, Mistress," he said.

"Very good," she said. "So, prove me right. Otherwise, you're calling me a liar."

She then picked up that riding crop and started over on him again, starting exactly as she had done before, only this time, she continued on for about an hour, putting him through hell as she did it. And just like before, she appeared to be in complete ecstasy the whole time she was torturing him. This time, however, he did not pass out, even though he really wished he could have.

When it was over, she went back to where she was before and wiped her hands again. "At least you weren't stupid enough to try to prove me a liar. I'd hate to cut off that thing of yours so early in our time together."

She stared at him intently, smiling as she realized he was practically crying. "When was the last time you came?"

"Mistress, I haven't cum since arriving here."

She started laughing. "My god, Mistress Cynthia is getting quite cruel. Someday, she might make a great dominatrix."

She then wandered back over to him and reached down behind him, unlocking the chain that was pulling his hands to the board behind him. She then unlocked his hands and pulled his right hand back down to where his legs were hooked to the platform, locking that wrist's manacle to the same hook.

His left hand, however, she grabbed and brought it in front of him, placing it right on his cock, and then she stepped back, staring at his cock. "Whack off."

David was surprised. He wasn't sure if she was serious.

"Either do it now or never get the chance again."

He started stroking his cock in front of her. Her eyes fixated on his actions. He realized he was probably seconds away from cumming. He was almost scared to stroke it.

"You have my permission to cum," she said.

It had to be a trick, he thought, but he continued stroking his cock. Then, he realized he was going to cum. His whole body was starting to convulse, preparing for the explosion.

Then he felt her hand on his wrist, pulling his hand away from cock. "Not fast enough." She pulled his hand to his side and locked the manacle to a hook in the contraption close to his left side, nowhere near his other hand, but nowhere close enough to where he could continue whacking off.

She smiled and continued to stare at his cock. "You still have permission to cum if you want."

David knew there was no way in the world he was going to be able to cum without at least one more real touch, and in this position he was not going to get it. He couldn't even use his legs to stimulate himself because the bonds kept his legs stretched far away from each other.

He thrashed against his bonds, but he could do nothing to finish off the chore. Instead, all he got in return was the laughter of Mistress Talia who seemed to enjoy the fact that he was so close but yet so far.

His body finally started calming down again.

She reached down and undid his wrist from the hook. "Cum."

He started stroking fast this time, convinced he would cum

before she stopped him, but as he got closer this time, he realized he was not going to be fast enough because she had his wrist in her hands again, forcing it into the shackle before he could finish the deed. He continued thrashing again, but nothing he could do would finish off the moment.

"This is so mean of me, isn't it?" she said with a pout. "Why is Mistress Talia being so mean to you?"

It was one of those questions not really requiring an answer. Mistress Talia was being mean because she loved to be mean. And he was the victim of the day, or the year for all he knew.

Then he calmed down again, and she unhooked him once more. "Come on, you're frustrating me. Cum!"

He started working harder this time, doing everything he could to cum before she stopped him. This time, he was really close, and sure enough, she grabbed his wrist and pulled it towards the shackle. He tried to fight back, just to give it that last stroke it would need before he felt the full force of Mistress Talia force his wrist back into place.

She stepped away from him and then grabbed the riding crop. "David, what was that?"

It hadn't even dawned on him what had just happened there until she asked him about it. He had fought back.

"Answer me, David," she said.

He knew there was no answer that would satisfy her here. He had fought back, and exhaustion, temporary insanity or even alien inhabitation was not going to be an applicable excuse. "Mistress, I am so sorry."

To his surprise, she perked up and spoke almost like a giddy little girl. "Okay, no problem." Then she undid his wrist again. "Come on, cum for me." Her hands were waving in front of her like this was an event of fun for all, and there was a gleeful look of mischievousness on her face.

It took him a second to get going again because he was still convinced she was angry with him for fighting back. Then he started one more time, all the time not sure of what to make of the dominatrix in front of him who seemed to be acting like a junior high school girl, bouncing up and down like this was her first sleepover. Then he forgot all about that and got back into trying to relieve himself before she stopped him. This time, it looked like he was going to make it. And then that damn hand came at him again, pulling his wrist until he was secured again.

She pouted again. "You just can't win, can you, Davey?"

His whole groin area was about to explode and he felt like someone had hit him with a pitchfork there. The tease and denial action was beginning to really hurt. And he knew she didn't care. Or that she did care, but not in any way that worked in his favor.

She stared at him for a long time, as the urgent need to ejaculate subsided. Then she went to remove his wrist from its captivity again. He knew that this could last all day, and she wouldn't get tired once. He was the only one being exhausted here.

She released his wrist and then backed away from him again. "What are you waiting for? You have my permission to cum."

He was about to give it up, but he knew that she would never allow that. At least, for a few moments, he was allowed a bit of pleasurable touching of himself, something he hadn't been allowed since arriving at this place. It was just so frustrating without the completion of the act.

He reached down and started stroking again, going really slow this time instead of jerking it hard like he had been doing before when he was trying to beat her to the orgasm before she stopped him. He continued slowly for a few moments until he noticed that she was just staring at him, her eyes glaring into his intently. This went on for a few moments until he actually realized he was about to cum. It was the same arching of his back, and his whole system appeared ready to explode down there, but he knew what was going to happen next; she was going to stop him and leave him frustrated even longer.

But it didn't happen this time. Instead, he exploded. Yes, that was probably the best description of what he did, and he'd never felt such great pleasure before in his lifetime. He'd cum many times before in the past, but not like this. It was like it was his very first time, and a fear told him it might just be the very last as well.

It lasted for nearly a few minutes before he realized that she was still staring at him, humor in her eyes. "Finished?"

For some reason, he felt really odd being chained up before her right after ejaculating all over the floor in front of her. It just didn't seem right, almost as if this was some kind of forbidden experience, and he would end up being punished for days as a result of this "mistake" of his.

She walked away from him, her eyes not leaving him once as

she did. She retrieved a towel and then tossed it to his left hand, the one still holding his penis. "Clean up."

He wiped himself up, but he couldn't reach the floor to clean up the mess he had made.

She grabbed the towel back from him. "Don't worry about that. I'll have someone take care of that later."

David felt like collapsing. He was exhausted from what had just happened. But he also realized that resting was something that wasn't allowable right now. He was limited to whatever Mistress Talia desired of him.

She locked his hand back with his other one behind his back. Then she walked over to a table in the room and came back with the hood from before. She shoved it over his head, securing it and then redoing the zipper and Velcro fastener over his mouth.

She said nothing to him. He wasn't sure if he had done something wrong, or what. Then he felt a tug on his penis, and he thought she was going to hurt him, but then he realized too late what was being done. She reattached the chastity device onto him. He was too spent from the moment before to have an erection so the device slipped right onto him and she quickly locked it in place.

"You cum only when I let you, remember that. Now that you've received pleasure from me, I intend to make sure that you understand what it is like to receive pain from me as well. You must learn to love only me, and by the time I am done with you, you won't even know another woman exists in the world. Or you will suffer. A lot."

Then he heard her walk out of the room and the huge door slam shut behind her. She didn't even lock it; it was obvious that he was not going anywhere.

Chapter XXI

Unlike previous times with Mistress Cynthia, Mistress Talia did not leave David alone for very long. She was gone for only a few hours, although David didn't know how long she was going to be. He only knew that he was chained very uncomfortably to this platform in this underground dungeon. Still, having had a look around at the different equipment in this dungeon, he figured that being chained uncomfortably had to be a lot better than what else she could do to him in this place.

But that wasn't even the problem that David was thinking about as he was left alone in this dungeon. The problem to him was that everything had suddenly changed. Just a short time ago, he signed over his life to Mistress Dominique who then gave him to Mistress Cynthia to train him to be the slave she desired. While it was mostly a living hell for him, at least it was something he knew he would have to endure in order to finally win the favor of the mistress to whom he intended to devote his life. Mistress Talia was a completely different issue.

There was probably not anyone involved with Mistress Dominique back then that did not know David was enthralled by Mistress Talia. It was more than just her beauty; it was nothing less than her philosophy of life and everything she stood for. She was tough, but she was also an extremist that seemed to embody everything David seemed to both fear and crave at the same time.

Before Mistress Talia, David actually believed he could do what was necessary to finally make Mistress Dominique believe he was the slave she desired. With Mistress Talia in the picture, David didn't know what might happen in the future. She was just the kind of woman who might throw everything out of kilter.

Her words also worried him. With Mistress Cynthia, the emphasis had always been on making sure that he learned to be the proper slave, so that he would eventually please Mistress Dominique. Mistress Talia seemed to have a different motive; she said she wanted him to be hers completely, to be the only woman to whom he would dedicate himself. This scared David because this didn't sound like something that benefited Mistress Dominique in any way, and he wasn't sure what he could do about it other than do everything possible to please Mistress Talia who didn't seem to be acting in the interests of Mistress Dominique, but through some personal motivation instead. And all he could do now was whatever she wanted because anything less would turn into a nightmare for him.

He wondered what she really wanted from him and why she needed to train him rather than Mistress Cynthia. With Mistress Cynthia, he was being trained to do exactly what would please Mistress Dominique. With Mistress Talia it made no sense. She seemed to be interested in him based on their interactions in the past, and for some reason David couldn't see how that would have any bearing on the future he had signed away to Mistress Dominique.

When Mistress Talia returned, David was still thinking about this dilemma, and then finally he realized that it really didn't matter what he thought about it because it was completely out of his control. He was a chained, naked slave in her dungeon; all that mattered was whatever she wanted from him.

"Miss me while I was gone?" she said after she re-entered the dungeon.

David knew she didn't want an answer so he didn't offer one.

"Our last moment together ended with your pleasure. Now, we need to focus on my pleasure. That's fair, isn't it?" He could hear her laugh as she thought about what she just said. "I'll bet that bondage is really uncomfortable on you. Let me free you from that."

She unlatched the chains holding him to the wooden platform and then forced him up to his feet. She then grabbed his left wrist and pulled him towards her, maneuvering him around the dungeon to another location. David tried to remember where he was in relation to where she was pulling him but then she started moving him around in circles until he had no idea what direction he was facing. Then she pushed him over a table and swung his legs up onto the table so he was lying flat. She then attached his ankle manacles to the bottom of the table and then began doing the same to his wrists at the top of the table. In a few moments, David was lying down on his back, tied to the table, waiting for whatever it was that Mistress Talia was going to do to him.

"Oh boy, Davey, you're tied to a table and completely vulnerable to the evil Mistress Talia. What do you think she's going to do next?"

David had no idea what was going to happen next.

Then he heard the sound of a ratchet as it started being turned, and his wrists started to be pulled further away from his feet. He was being stretched on a rack.

"Oh no! Poor Davey is being stretched by the evil Mistress Talia!" She was laughing as she said it.

It only took a few seconds before David started to feel real pressure in his arms as they were pulled to a point that the stretching was now affecting his entire body. And she continued stretching him, his body tightening more and more as she turned the ratchet continuously.

The gear she was turning made a horrible sound of metal clanking each time she turned it, and she would turn it for a few seconds, stretching him and then stop for a moment. Then she would continue again, that metal clanking indicating that he was being stretched even further, even though the uncomfortable sensation going through his body told him that just as well. And she would start and stop over and over, much like she did before when she was allowing him to masturbate.

"Does it hurt yet, Davey?" she said.

It actually did not hurt yet. Well, not that badly. "No, Mistress," he said.

"Wonderful!" she said. For some reason, he imagined Mistress Talia twirling around the room dancing as she said what she did. But then the metal clanking started up again. As his arms started to stretch further, all thoughts of a happy mistress dancing around the room immediately dissipated. All he could focus on was the fact that the ratcheting sound kept continuing, and his body was stretching further and further.

After a few minutes of this, with real slow stretching, David was beginning to feel real pain from what she was doing to him. He had been stretched before, but this was reaching a point where he was starting to fear that his arms were going to be pulled out of their sockets.

"Is it hurting yet, Davey?" she said.

"Yes, Mistress," he said, and he definitely wasn't lying.

"Too bad," she replied and she turned the ratchet again.

The pain was extremely uncomfortable, and it was the kind of pain that just kept on adding and adding because the situation causing it was still acting upon his body. Yet, there was nothing he could do about it but just take it.

"This is so much fun, Davey. We should have done it a long time ago."

Her voice was coming from his right side. Then he felt an intense pain from his left leg as she hit him with what felt like a cane. Then she hit his other leg and then continued up and down his body with the cane, drawing blood several times with very good hits.

Then she stopped. David prepared himself for yet another round of pain, but surprisingly, it did not come.

"It's only our first day together, David. I would like you to take some time to reflect on the future we are going to have together. I'll come back for you when I think you're ready to continue your lessons."

Then he heard her walk to the door and it slam shut behind her. He was left alone, locked down on the rack of her prison, left to contemplate his existence under her spell.

David had no idea how long it was before Mistress Talia returned, but after what appeared to be a very long time, with him not even able to thrash in his bonds due to the intense stretching, he heard the sound of her boots outside in the hallway and then the sound of the huge door being opened and closed behind her. Then he heard her walk over to him and then stop, remaining completely silent, possibly standing over him and just watching to see what kind of reaction he might make.

As strange as it seemed, even though David was wearing a hood over his head, he had a suspicion that if he gave the wrong facial expression or reaction to Mistress Talia, she still would have known about it. He was in one of those states of being that no one can ever truly understand, and he was in it with a woman who seemed to understand him more than he probably understood himself. There was no way around anything she might do to him, and there was probably no way of keeping anything from her as well. He had learned a long time ago that no matter how you try to put one over on one's mistress, a seasoned mistress always seems to know what's going on before the slave can get away with whatever discretion was attempted. And he suspected this time was going to be no different.

The heat of her fingers ran from his neck and caressed him in a slow motion down the rest of his body until she came to his chastity device. There she stopped and ran circles around the contraption that kept him from gaining any type of pleasure that she might be willing to offer. Then she started to pull at the bonds of the chastity device, running her fingers under the straps, pulling it back and forth before snapping it back to its resting place; then she continued moving up and down his body with her exploring fingers.

"Have you given any thought to what I was saying earlier?" she said as he fingers continued to do their exploration of his body.

He didn't know what to answer, so he said nothing. He figured she would probably punish him for his silence, but he had no idea what she was talking about, and he felt that even with an answer, he was probably going to be punished anyway.

But she obviously wasn't looking for an answer. "How long have you been thinking of me, Davey? After I disappeared from you life, did I disappear from your thoughts as well? Or have you been dreaming about me like I think you have been?" Those hands kept moving up and down his body. "You've been fantasizing about me, haven't you?" There was a strong hint of humor in her voice as she spoke.

He had been fantasizing about her, for about as long as he could remember. When she first started messing with his mind while he was Mistress Dominique's houseboy, he was fascinated with her. When she left the employ of Mistress Dominique, he started fantasizing about her even more, wondering what it might have been like if he had actually become her slave instead of the slave of Mistress Dominique. There were times that he suspected that the disappearance of Mistress Talia from the house was partially because of, or mainly because of, Mistress Dominique's desire for control over him. But every time that he thought things like that, he realized how stupid it sounded because both women were so in demand by so many submissives that such thoughts were ridiculous, if not outright stupid.

"I asked you a question, slave," was the voice that brought him back into reality again. Then he felt the Velcro over his mouth being pulled away from the hood. "I expect an answer."

He took a deep breath and then let it out. "Yes, Mistress, I have thought about you a lot."

She started laughing. "And what exactly have you been thinking about me, slave?"

He really didn't want to answer her. It was embarrassing,

and it just didn't seem to be right considering the fact that Mistress Dominique now owned him. "Mistress, I often thought about being owned by you."

The laughter continued. "And what exactly did you think it would be like?"

"I don't know, Mistress. For some reason I could never figure that out."

She laughed for a while this time. "Then you have truly been thinking about me. Being owned by me is never knowing what is going to happen to you next."

Then he felt her reach down and replace the Velcro over his mouth again. Then he heard the sound of her boots as she walked around the rack he was on. She stopped on the other side of him and then he felt her hand move up his chest to the hood. "As I was saying, you can never tell what is going to happen to you next."

Then he felt her hand close around his mouth and then her other hand grasp over his nose. Then both hands closed in, and immediately his ability to breathe stopped. He hadn't even been expecting it, and he had very little air in his system when it happened.

David started thrashing immediately, realizing that she wasn't going to give him the chance to breathe. Yet, his thrashing did nothing to change what she was doing. From the pressure she was exerting, his thrashing appeared to just make her grasp him even harder. As he tried to fight against his very secure bondage to at least give himself a moment to take in a breath, he realized the bonds of the rack weren't going to make that possible, and then he heard a sound that made him realize how little mercy she was willing to give him: she started laughing.

"You can't fight me, Davey," she said. "Men much tougher than you have been nothing more than victims to me. You have little chance of being anything more." And then she started laughing, almost hysterically. "But it's so much damn fun when you try. You make this so much fun."

David realized struggling against her hands wouldn't really do anything to end the torment she was putting him through. This was a woman who put men through this all of the time; his chances of succeeding against her were beyond slim. They were almost impossible. But even though he knew he couldn't succeed against her, he couldn't help but fight against her because his lack of breathing made it so he could do nothing but fight against it. The fact that it was bringing plea-sure to her probably meant that she was only going to make it worse on him.

This seemed to go on forever, and then his head began to swim. And then it started to hurt. Then he felt her hand move away from his mouth and he gasped, air actually coming into his mouth. The sweet taste of oxygen was a wonderful sensation.

She pulled the Velcro fastener from his mouth and then he found himself able to breathe much clearer than before. He felt relieved because it seemed as if she was finished with controlling his breathing. And then, if he had not been chained to a rack, he would have slapped himself for being so stupid and predictable because he felt her fiddle with the mouth opening of the hood and then realized she was pushing something through the opening. It was the end of a tube, and she forced it into his mouth. And then she forced it deep into his mouth to where it was almost about to be forced down his throat, but stopped right before it broke the barrier leading into his throat.

He was scared to death. He had no idea what she was doing.

But he also realized he could breathe through the tube, and then he also realized that if she cut off his breathing by stopping up the end of the tube, he could probably breathe around the tube as it did not seal around his mouth. At least that's what he thought until he heard the sound of a valve being turned on the table itself. It only took the first flow of water into his mouth for him to realize that she was turning a water valve, and the tube was emptying water into his mouth.

His mouth filled up quickly, but the water continued pouring into his mouth in a slow, steady manner so that he couldn't just spit it out and try to breathe through his mouth again. He found himself choking on the water, and started to go through convulsions.

"Breathe through your nose, David," she said. "Don't swallow the water. I'd hate for you to have to die so soon after I started really torturing you."

He did what she told him, even though it was so hard to change his breathing to his nose as the hood over his head made it so that very little fresh air seemed to be coming into his respiratory system. Yet, he also realized, after he started choking on the water again, that he really didn't have any choice. It was either change his breathing to his nose, or die. Somehow, even though he knew that Mistress Talia wasn't here to kill him, he kind of doubted that she was going to give him a third option aside from breathing through his nose and dying.

"Very good, slave," she said. "Breathe slowly. Get used to the rhythm of the water and your breathing. And remember that Mistress Talia is here for you, and I would never let anything happen to you." Then she leaned close to him so that she was speaking into his right ear, loud enough so that the muffled voice still managed to be comforting through the leather hood. "Breathe in," she said and then waited a moment. "Breathe out." A long moment. "Breathe in." And then: "Breathe out." She continued this way for a long time until he found himself in a continuous pattern that followed her instructions.

For some reason, he voice sounded so smooth and reassuring. With the constant flow of water and the slow breathing he was doing, he began to feel comfortable in her presence. And that was right about the time that he realized she was plugging his nose again.

He thrashed around again, and this time realized that as he tried to breathe in, he was choking in water at the same time, and water ran up his nose in the process, causing him to spasm even more. He felt like he was dying from being unable to breathe and drowning at the same time. Meanwhile, the only sound he could hear was giggling and laughter from Mistress Talia.

This went on for what appeared to be forever, and David was beginning to think he was really going to die. And then she removed her hands from his nose, and he could breathe again. His nose really hurt, and his throat ached, and his head was pounding over and over. Then she did it again. This time it seemed to be even longer than the last time, and he was somewhat wishing he could die, but he knew that was one thing she would never allow him. He was under her power for as long as she wanted him to be her slave.

When he could breathe again, she spoke to him. "Davey, I want you to think in your thoughts about me every time that I do this to you. When you cannot breathe, I want you to remember your life before you became a slave. That is what your life used to represent. When I release you, you are to think of me, of your love for me, and to understand that it is my love for you that allows you to breathe during those times that I stop hurting you. Let's try it again."

She plugged up his nose, and like usual, she caught him completely by surprise. He tried to struggle against her, and even though he realized his struggles would do no good, he knew he could do nothing but fight her, as much of a losing cause as that happened to be.

But as he struggled, he could hear the soft whispering of her beautiful voice.

"Davey, think of the life you just gave up, the times of having no one caring for you, no woman controlling your actions, the total freedom of loneliness that you were experiencing. Think of working for some guy you never liked, who treated you in a way that never even hinted at your true value, meanwhile you knew how much potential you really had, how you could make a woman extremely happy and satisfied, but you had no way of making it happen. Think on that."

And then she left him thinking about it, saying nothing. He struggled against the situation she put him into, and he realized he was thinking of her words, even though his real need was to breathe, but he knew there was no way he would be able to breathe until she let him, and all he could do was think about what she ordered him to think about.

And then he could breathe again.

"Now, imagine that you have been taken over by me, your mistress. I mean the world to you. I offer you the opportunity to be what your other world can never allow you. I am your mistress, your owner, and I am your entire life. I give you the ability to breathe. I am everything to you. Do you understand me, slave?"

He nodded, as it was impossible for him to say anything through the tube and a mouth filled with water.

"Now, remember that horrible life of yours again," she said as she plugged up his nose again. After he started struggling, she began speaking to him. "You're in that horrible life again. It's a world without me. It's a world without an owner telling you what to do. There is no air for you here. There is no Mistress Talia providing you with the sweet taste of oxygen that you so much want, that you need, that you would give everything to have at this moment. Think about it, young man. When I speak to you again, you will be able to breathe again because my love, my power over you, is the beauty that offers you air and life. Remember that."

And then she stopped speaking, and he thrashed back and forth in what little room he had available to him, but he couldn't breathe no matter what he did. Then, finally, she released his nose, and the air came flowing into his lungs again.

"Remember, slave, that air you are breathing comes from me. Without me, your mistress, you have no air, but you have received it as a gift from me. Remember how wonderful this feels and who made it possible for you."

He knew this was all some type of mind control she was using on him, but even though he was aware of this, he couldn't help but feel grateful to her for allowing him to breathe again. And he was beginning to feel exactly what she told him each time she stopped him from breathing, and each time she allowed him to breathe again, even though he knew how manufactured these thoughts were, manufactured by a woman who was providing his thoughts for him, while at the same time providing the suffering that should have made him fear her rather than respect and worship her.

This continued for a number of times, with her plugging his breathing and then making him realize how it was old life while he was suffering. Then she would provide him with air and then remind him how it was her control over him that allowed him the pleasure of life again. For David, it was very hard not to accept that Mistress Talia was a wonderful woman for providing him with air when he so needed it. After a few more rounds of this, he was practically putty in her hands.

Then he heard the sound of the valve being turned again. The water stopped flowing into his mouth. After a moment, he felt her pull the tube from his mouth.

"You may swallow the water and then breathe through your mouth again, slave," she said.

He gulped down the water and then took his first breath through his mouth again. He had almost forgotten how nice it was to breathe through that orifice.

"Tell me your thoughts, slave," said Mistress Talia.

He wasn't sure what to say. He was exhausted, but somehow he knew that his state of exhaustion was not what Mistress Talia wanted to hear from him. "Mistress, I am very thankful for the opportunity to breathe again."

"That's it?" she said. "Not a testament to how much you want me, how much you need me, how much you love me? Tell me I am the only mistress you will ever love."

He realized he couldn't say this, as much as he wanted to say it just to please Mistress Talia. He hesitated and thought about it for a second.

"Too late," she said. "You don't love me yet. But you will. I promise you that."

Then she sealed up his mouth again with the Velcro and he could hear the boots on the floor of the cell as she walked away from him. Then there was the sound of the huge door being closed, and he was left in silence.

Chapter XXII

He felt like she left him alone forever this time. His arms were in serious pain, and that was so long ago that the pain started that he had no idea how long he was tied to the rack. And he realized that it really didn't matter to Mistress Talia. This place was not designed around a man's limits; the only limits were the ones that were placed upon him, and they usually involved the limits of a woman's mercy. From his experience, there didn't appear to be a lot of mercy here.

He was drifting in between reality and a dream state. It was so hard to get sleep when in such pain and such controlled arousal, but he was most definitely exhausted. He so much wanted to sleep, but no matter how hard he tried, he was only able to manage a few moments at a time, and with the hood on, it was hard to tell when he was actually sleeping and when he was just suffering while awake.

Then he heard the sound of the door as it was pulled open. Then the footsteps into the room.

As usual, David was scared whenever someone came into a room where he was. It was always painful and an experience filled with suffering. He waited for the words of Mistress Talia, wondering if he could ascertain what type of day it would be by the tone of how she addressed him at the start of their day together.

"How are you, slave?" she said.

"Mistress, my body really, really hurts," he said, even though he realized she probably didn't care that much for how he felt.

However, Mistress Talia's response was not a verbal one. Instead, she wandered to the other side of the rack and began to turn the ratchet. Slowly, his arms and legs began to lose the stretching tension. She only moved the ratchet a few times, but he could immediately feel the difference in his arms and legs when the stretching lessened.

But it was surprisingly quite painful as she left him stretched in the new position, not as stretched as before, but with his body at a new level of stretching that he was not used to. Shockingly, it was not as far of a stretch as before, but it was a new sense of pain.

After he began to adjust to the present state of pain, she turned the ratchet a few times again, and the stretching lessened again. Again, the pain, but a new sensation of it as it was a stretch at a different position.

This went on for quite some time until he realized that he was no longer stretched. He was now just tied down and lying on his back, even though it took him awhile to figure out that he was no longer being stretched.

To his surprise, the next thing Mistress Talia did to him was start to rub his arms and legs, massaging them up and down over and over again. Slowly, the feeling started to come back to him, even though he felt serious pain in his arms and legs. Still, she continued to rub them continuously so that more and more feeling came back to him.

"I'll bet it feels wonderful to be free from that," said Mistress Talia. "Tell me, slave. How do you feel now?"

"Mistress, it feels so much better. It still hurts a lot, but thank you, Mistress, so much for freeing me from that."

"You're welcome, slave. I have much for you to do today. Can't have you lying around all day."

Somehow, that revelation didn't make him feel very good.

Mistress Talia undid the bonds on his wrists and then sat him up on the rack. While his ankles were still attached to the lower end of the rack, she grabbed his wrists and pulled them behind his back, attaching a lock onto the two wrist restraints so that his hands were locked behind his back.

She then undid the restraints on his ankles and swung him to a side so that he was sitting over the side of the rack and then attached a small chain to the two ankle restraints so that his ankles were locked close together.

"Stand up, slave," she said.

Carefully, he tried to maneuver himself off the rack's surface onto the floor, and even though he realized he was probably going collapse when his feet hit the floor, he knew better than to not do as Mistress Talia ordered or to make her wait. But, to his surprise, he felt Mistress Talia hold him up as his feet hit the floor, holding him so he didn't fall to the floor.

"Come with me, slave," she said as she maneuvered him towards the door. He walked across the stone floor for quite some time until she stopped him without saying a word. He heard the sound of a large cell door opening and then she came back to him and ushered him into the cell.

He figured she was putting him back into solitary confinement like he had experienced when first coming to this part of the prison. Instead, she forced him to his knees and then pushed him forward until he realized he was being pushed into a very small cage. The door to the cage was so small, he found it very hard to fit into it, but with a series of kicks that came from his mistress, he found himself pushed into the tiny cage. Once inside, she closed the cage door behind him and he heard the sound of locking mechanism.

He found himself barely able to move once inside the cage. His back was almost touching the top of the cage, and he was touching both the front and back of it with his head and feet, indicating that it was a very tiny cage. There were bars all across the cage and a metallic surface that filled the floor of the space. There was very, very little room to maneuver in the cage, even if his hands weren't secured behind his back. He doubted that even with his freedom to move available to him, he wouldn't have been able to turn around in this space.

"I find this very symbolic between us, slave," said Mistress Talia. "This is almost how we started together. Do you remember the first cage I saw you in?"

How could he forget? She threatened him on that day and remained in his fantasies ever since.

"I am going to leave you here for some time," she said. "I want you to think of nothing but me. Think of how much you want to be my slave. Remember that I am the only woman who can give you what you so desperately want in your life. Think about that as I leave you alone here." There was a long pause, but there was no sound of her boots leaving the cell. "This is how you should always be," she added. "You were made to live in a cell, and I was made to keep you in one. I may never let you leave, slave. Think about that."

And then he heard her boots and then the larger cell door being sealed behind her.

So he crouched in the cage of the prison cell for a long time, waiting for Mistress Talia to come back and decide what she was going to do with him next. For some reason, even though the idea of being locked in a cell was always a great fantasy for him, all he could really think about was the fact that he was beginning to really hate this hood that he was forced to wear on his head. Mistress Talia was a beautiful woman, and it seemed too unfair to be tortured constantly by her and never be able to see her. It was almost as if all of that beauty was being put to waste.

Being in a cage used to be a wonderful experience for him, and it was something Mistress Dominique used to love to inflict upon him. She used to love to make him write in a journal to her, to detail his every thought to her, and then she would come back and read his words while he was locked in the cage that she was sitting outside of, analyzing his words, deciding what to do next with him.

For David, it gave him an opportunity to think about what kind of life this would be for him. For many hours, he remembered fantasizing about what life would be like if he could be put through slavery 24/7. They were such rich fantasies, and they usually involved exactly what kind of slavery he was living at the time, but with much more of a permanence to the situation added. He never actually imagined what it would be like if it really happened to him, which is what was happening to him now. Actually, it was what had already happened to him, and now he was just living through it.

This time, however, as he crouched in this cell, he no longer had fantasies about what would happen if this became real because it already was real. The woman who put him into the cell wasn't offering him an opportunity to make this all real, and he didn't have to do any convincing to make this all become real. He was locked in a cell by a very sadistic woman who already had complete control over him, and it was something that was going to remain this way for a very long time.

He even suspected that his signed contract was for a duration as long as this woman intended to keep it, even though he didn't even sign the contract with this particular woman to begin with.

His thoughts had little to do with what his old fantasies used to be when he used to be locked in a cage by a beautiful woman. Reality has a bad habit of doing that to someone's fantasies.

Then he heard the main cell door unlock and then open again. The boots entered the cell and walked over to where he was. It was Mistress Talia, and she spoke.

"You do realize that I can do anything I want with you now, don't you?" She started laughing again. "There's something I want you to think about, and believe me, all you have is time to think in your situation. I want you to think about what it is I mean to you. What is it you want for the rest of your life as a slave? And more importantly, have you ever considered being my slave, and my slave alone?"

He said nothing. He wasn't sure if she wanted a response, but he really couldn't think of an answer to that one that wouldn't piss off Mistress Talia. He already sold his soul to another woman; he was only temporarily under Mistress Talia's control at the discretion of his real mistress.

"I want you to think about this, slave. Right now, I own you. Your life is mine. I can do anything I want to you, and if I want, I never have to release you out of my control. I am the one obstacle you have to get past, and if you don't get my approval, you remain my victim for the rest of your life. But I could make it much easier on you. I could make you my personal slave, and I could have you serve just me as my true slave. Don't try to tell me you haven't thought about it before."

He definitely didn't know what to say.

"I'm going to leave you here for awhile," she said. "When I come back, I want an answer from you. Either you choose to be my slave for life, or I'll make your life miserable for as long as you live. Either way, you'll be mine. But one of those choices allows you the chance to actually be a cherished slave rather than nothing more than my worthless victim." And then she started laughing again. "But honestly, either choice is fine with me. Either way, you'll never taste freedom again."

And then she left.

Chapter XXIII

Mistress Talia left David in a state where he was very uncomfortable, but it was not just a lack of comfort in his surroundings, but in what he had to think about. He knew that Mistress Dominique owned him; while he often fantasized about Mistress Talia in the past, he also knew that it just wasn't something that was meant to be. But at the same time, he also didn't realize any way out of this situation. He doubted other slaves that came through this place had to deal with a history with the prison guard before they met her. Most probably suffered extensively and then went to wherever it was they were destined to go in the first place. He doubted any had to deal with a slightly psychotic mistress who would not take no for an answer.

And the difficult part of it all was that he did desire Mistress Talia. He desired her for many years. She was one of the most beautiful women he had ever known, and she was essentially the opposite of what Mistress Dominique was. Mistress Dominique was the loving dominant, the sensual one, who always made him feel that his submission to her really meant something. Mistress Talia was the bitch from Hell who showed no mercy and would use her intense, exotic beauty to wear down a man until there was no way he could resist her. Both were equally powerful and cruel when they wanted and needed to be, but while Mistress Dominique was stern and strict, but loving, Mistress Talia was just outright mean. And surprisingly, even though David was not what one would consider a masochist, that was damn sexy in a woman to almost any type of submissive.

But before he could even run every scenario through his mind, he heard the door open again, and Mistress Talia was back. "Well, slave, I gave you a few hours. How have you decided to spend the rest of your life?"

He was almost scared to answer. He really didn't want to be tortured again by this woman, but at the same time he had a vow, and he couldn't go against it. It would make him a complete fake, and as strange as it seemed, it was the one thing he had left in his own control, and that was his original decision to become Mistress Dominique's slave. If he lived up to his responsibilities, he really didn't even have the option to make yet another decision about deciding his own future. It was decided a long time ago when he first decided to come to this place, or to wherever it was Mistress Dominique wanted to send or take him.

"Having a hard time still?" she said. "How about if I sweeten the pot for you? I want you as my personal slave. That means that you will serve me exclusively. Whenever I want something, you will be my slave to deliver it. If I want a victim, you will be that victim. If I want sex, you'll be my sexual plaything. You will have everything a slave has ever wanted from his mistress. And you will have my strictness and control. Never will you ever have to question yourself about anything. I will decide everything in your life from this moment forward. And to answer your question about how you will have to break this to Mistress Dominique, once you accept my proposal, I will whisk you out of here, and you will be mine forever. She will never even know what happened to you." He felt her soft hand on his back, caressing it back and forth. "So, slave, are you ready to explore your life the way it was meant to be?"

He took a deep breath and let it out. "Mistress Talia, I wish I could say yes. Oh God, do I wish I could say yes. But I offered my freedom to Mistress Dominique. I can't betray that oath I made to her."

There was a long pause where nothing was said, and for a moment, David actually thought he felt the temperature drop ten degrees. Then she spoke. "David, I offered you everything, and you spit in my face. Do you have any idea how your life is about to be from this moment forward? Do you even suspect the level of punishment I am willing to dole out to you as a result of going against my wishes? Fine. Honor your oath, but understand that your days are completely numbered from this moment forward."

He could hear the sound of the cage being opened, and then he felt her dragging him out of the cage. She stood him up onto his feet. "Follow me, slave. No more niceness for you."

She led him into the hallway and then threw him to the stone floor, catching his head as he was falling so that he didn't crack open his skull. He was quickly lying on his stomach, feeling her remove the lock from his wrist restraints. "Put your arms at your side, slave."

He did. He also had no idea what was going to happen, but he was not looking forward to what was going to happen to him.

"I am going to give you the benefit of the doubt and assume that you are just scared. I am going to ask you one more time if you want to be my slave. When I ask you, it will be your very last opportunity, and then the suffering I am going to start now will continue until you breathe your last breath. Understand that."

He said nothing.

"You have been idle in this place too long. Do you think that slaves are supposed to be catered to by their mistresses? Do you?"

"No, Mistress," he said.

"Shut the fuck up, slave!" she said. "I don't want to hear from you. I don't care about anything you have to say. If I want your opinion, or even an answer, I will beat it out of you. Understand that. Now, let's see if we can get you a little more active. Push-ups! Now!"

It took him a bit by surprise, but he moved into position to do push-ups. But obviously, he was not quick enough because he felt the sting of a riding crop as it hit him squarely across his behind. Quickly, he began doing push-ups.

He did about twenty push-ups before she spoke. "Stop immediately! I will tell you when to do them, and you will do them to my count only! Now, when I say ONE, you will go down to the ground and then push yourself all the way up. If you have pleased me, we will go onto TWO. Now, ONE!"

He dropped down to his stomach and then pushed himself up off the ground.

"What the hell was that? Trying out for the Special Olympics? ONE!"

He tried again.

"Not even close, slave," she said. "ONE!"

He tried to be very straight this time, and did another push-up, holding himself up when he was done.

"TWO!"

He did another one.

"TWO!"

Gritting his teeth, he tried to do another very good push-up. She then moved onto three.

This went on for a while, and after he reached about ten, she started to use the riding crop on him every time a push-up wasn't exactly to her standards. And they never were. And he was beginning to get very tired as well. No matter how hard he tried, he could not please her.

She was on twenty-four when she said something that scared him to no end. "You are going to reach two hundred before we're done here today."

He was already exhausted, and they were only at twenty-four. So she continued to order him to do more push-ups, even at his point of exhaustion, and she seemed to take great pleasure in striking him whenever he didn't make it through a proper one that met her standards of satisfaction. This went on for a very long time until he dropped to his stomach, too exhausted to push out yet another one. Then she started hitting him over and over again with the riding crop, ordering him to continue, even though he knew he couldn't do another one, even if his life depended on it, although he half suspected that it probably did.

"You disgust me," she said. "Turn over on your back."

He struggled and managed to get over onto his back.

"Sit-ups, now!"

He waited for her to begin counting. "ONE!"

He bent his knees and then managed to force himself up into a sit-up position. Instead of "two", he received a response of laughter from her. "You are kidding me, right? If that's how you're going to be doing sit-ups, I might as well just skin you alive right here and now."

So she continued to force him to do sit-ups, and he managed to get her to twelve before he fell exhausted, probably having done nearly seventy of them before she stopped him with another condemnation of how lousy his service was to her.

"Stand up," she said, as David, a heap of exhaustion on the floor, tried to stand up. She grabbed him by the ring loop in his collar and dragged him behind her into another room. There, she pushed him over a horizontal beam of some sort and then linked a lock from the restraints on his wrists to the restraints on his ankles. His behind was pointing up into the air.

Then she started hitting his behind with a leather strap over and over again. There was nothing David could do but just take it. And Mistress Talia was the kind of woman who liked to dish it out.

Then she walked across the room and came back, hitting him again across the buttocks, this time with what was obviously a cane. She hit him over and over again, drawing blood with almost every hit. She continued for a long time, with David screaming into his hood, begging her to stop, even though he knew that he was forbidden to say anything to her at any time. Sometimes, like this particular time, the pain was just too much not to say anything.

Then she stopped, wandered to the other side of the room again and came back with another item, hitting him with it immediately. It was a flat leather paddle whip that she hit him with over and over again. He was quickly screaming in pain. And her only responses were to hit him more and to laugh and giggle as she did.

Then she came back with a whip that had lots of straps hanging from it. She began hitting him all over his body with the implement, in some places causing a bit of pleasure by softly hitting him with it and then just unleashing its fury on other parts of his body. She knew exactly where and when to hit him so that he rarely had a moment of rest before she made him remember just how miserable his life really was.

This went on for hours with the only rest being a moment for Mistress Talia to grab another device of horror in which to use on poor David. And it never stopped.

Finally, after David was exhausted and slumped over the beam, realizing that he was resigned to the fact that his life was at an all-time low and that it would probably never get better, Mistress Talia wandered over to the other side of the room to grab another instrument of pain.

For the first time, David wondered if it might be worth it just to tell Mistress Talia whatever she wanted just to get her to stop. He was never designed for this. He was not a masochist; he was a service slave who loved to serve a beautiful woman and make her life much more enjoyable. This was never anything he really wanted, other than in his fantasies, and they were much better as fantasies because no one ever really wanted to live like this, at least not to this extent. Well, some people probably did, but certainly not David. This was nothing less than living in Hell, and he realized he was not cut out for it.

If she asked him right at this moment if he would become her slave and only her slave, he would have probably said yes. He wanted this to stop so much. He really wished he had not signed that contract; Mistress Dominique never told him it would be anything like this. She made it sound so sensual and wonderful when the two of them talked about it together. No one ever mentioned a raging lunatic with an assortment of whips and a lot of desire to use each and every one of them.

Yet, she continued. This time, she found a paddle and used it to pound on him over and over, laughing as she made the hits sound like some type of rhythmic melody she was putting together. "Can't you just hear the crescendo?" she said to no one in particular.

Then she stopped. She ran her fingers over the large bruises and blood that had to be all over his body. And she moved her fingers softly, presenting what was the first soft touch he'd received from her in quite some time.

"David, this is my last chance for you. Become my slave, and all of this stops now. You will become my personal live-in slave, and your life will be everything you've ever imagined it to be. Turn me down now, and this will never end. Never."

He said nothing.

"Answer now, slave," she said. "Do you choose me, or the woman who hasn't even seen you since you've been here? Mistress Talia or Mistress Dominique?"

He found himself breathing heavily. "Mistress Talia, I truly wish I could become your slave. I've fantasized about you for so long. But I love Mistress Dominique, even though I've not seen her but once since I've been here. She cared about me enough to put me through all of this so I could be the best slave I could ever be for her. While I may never see her because you choose to make it that way, I would never go against her desires or my promise to her. You can torture me to my very last breath, if that's what you desire, but I can never go against the only promise I have made in this life that I refuse to ever break."

The response he received was complete silence. He expected something stronger in condemnation, but instead he heard footsteps walk across the room to retrieve yet another implement. When she came back, she hit him with the new whip. To his surprise, it was a whip that felt a lot like a bunch of feathers. It didn't hurt, nor even tickle, but it felt remarkably nice on his body.

"You have done well," she said.

It only took David an instant to realize that the voice was not the voice of Mistress Talia. It was the voice of Mistress Dominique.

He felt a tug on the hood and all the straps were loosened. Then it was pulled off his face.

He found himself staring at the immortal beauty of Mistress Dominique who was standing next to Mistress Talia. There were smiles on both of their faces.

"He has passed the final test," said Mistress Talia to Mistress Dominique, "as you have seen yourself. I turn him back over to you, fully trained."

Mistress Dominique nodded and then waved off Mistress Talia who turned and smiled at David and then wandered out of the room. Mistress Dominique turned back to David and caressed his skin with the feathery whip. "I bet you thought you were never going to see me again, didn't you?"

David just stared at her, not sure of what to say.

She just laughed. "You have my permission to speak, David," she said. "I promise not to hurt you."

"Yes, Mistress, I thought I would never see you again."

"I figured Mistress Talia would be the final step in your training. If you could get past her, you were worthy of truly serving me."

"It's finally over, Mistress?" David said, still convinced some other shoe was still yet to fall.

"No, David," she said. "It's only the beginning. But it's going to be a wonderful experience."

She then reached forward and tightly hugged her slave. "I'm so proud of you, David." Then she wandered to the other wall, the wall where Mistress Talia had been getting implements of pain to use on him. "So many choices," she said as she stared at the wall and then back at her slave in bondage. "And so much time."

About the Author

Nigel Cross is a political scientist who lives in Stockton, California. Previously, he was a counter-intelligence agent and a creator of computer games.

Other Books By Nigel Cross
(written as Duane Gundrum)

Innocent Until Proven Guilty
Thompson's Bounty

Available at Amazon.com

www.ingramcontent.com/pod-product-compliance
Lightning Source LLC
Chambersburg PA
CBHW071217260626
47162CB00004B/1329